"I have never let my schooling interfere with my education."

—Mark Twain

About *Stella Maris and the Venice Beach Diaries*

You think you had a rotten day? Stella Maris was let go from her job, evicted, and dumped by her long-term boyfriend—all before lunch— it was her birthday. But plucky Stella clears out the joint account and hops the first flight to America. Finally several layovers and plane changes later, she arrives at her aunt's apartment in Venice Beach at midnight—to trip over a dead body. Thus begins an often-hilarious romp through the lives of the quirky denizens of Billy's Apartments and Venice Beach.

Stella may be a "stranger in a strange land" but between a little help from new friends, artist Olivia, attorney Mr. Bernstein, Liz the nextdoor neighbor, and Mr. Velvet the cat, she thrives amidst a funeral, a witches' bonfire, an attack, a missing boa constrictor, and the puzzling diaries. I fell in love with this zany book and its delightful characters. You'll think you're right there at the beach with them. I did. She's an unlikely heroine you'll cry with, laugh with, and root for from page one to the end. Author Aletheia Morden has hit it out of the beach volleyball court!

Ana Manwaring, recipient of the Literay Titan Gold Book Award for *Saints and Skeletons* and author of *The JadeAnne Stone Mexico Adventure Stories*.

ISBN 979-8-9897133-1-8

Library of Congress Control Number: 2025931939

Author's website: aletheiawrites.bravesites.com

Published by Canyon Rose Press
Benicia, California

Book design: Jan Malin

Printed in the United States of America

Stella Maris and the Venice Beach Diaries

A Novel With Dead Bodies

Aletheia Morden

He knew he shouldn't be doing this, but the midnight sea was so inviting. Night swimming was prohibited on Venice Beach. Still, he dove into the surf and swam out to the horizon. The moon was full; the ocean like the lens of a giant eye, a black iris in the moonlight. Turning on his back, he looked up at the stars. Young and far away from home, the night sky comforted him with its familiar constellations. He lay there, drifting in the warm current, feeling the silvery slither of fish against his legs.

Then he turned and started swimming towards the beach where he had left his clothes. But something was wrong. Instead of getting closer the shoreline was receding. Street lamps on the Boardwalk bobbed away from him becoming pinpricks of light instead of beacons.

His arms felt tired, his breath started to hurt. He panicked as he felt himself being dragged further out to sea by the current, which had turned colder. He tried calling for help, getting mouthfuls of salt water as he drifted out of the moonlight and into the shadows of the vast Pacific Ocean.

As the swimmer struggled in the riptide, someone stood on the dark shore watching. Fool! He'd been warned. Signs were posted everywhere. No one was supposed to be on the beach even when the grunion were running. The watcher stood for a while as the tide surged onto the beach casting dozens of fish in a silvery carpet.

Females dug straight down with their tails depositing coral-colored eggs into the sand. Males piled on top of each female, their milt running down her body fertilizing the eggs before the next wave would take them back out to sea in the million-year-old ritual peculiar to this coastline. In wave after wave they came and went.

The watcher's eyes lifted to the dark horizon; the feeble cries for help had faded. Bending down and shouldering the swimmer's backpack, the watcher walked back across the beach to the Boardwalk, throwing the swimmer's clothes and tennis shoes into a trash can.

CHAPTER I

Across a continent and another ocean, Stella Maris stood by the living-room window staring off into the distance towards the grassy slopes of the Sussex Downs where a flock of sheep nibbled its way across the horizon. *Sometimes I think about things too much, and sometimes I don't think very much at all.* Right now she was having trouble thinking much at all. It had been a disastrous day. Stella had been laid off her job that morning and had arrived home soon after to a notice from Brighton Borough Council taped to the front door announcing that the two up, two down Victorian row house she and her boyfriend Brian rented, was being sold. The whole area was being demolished and gentrified to make room for high rise blocks of luxury flats, the notice stated. That was upsetting, but she and Brian could find something else, Stella thought, perhaps even buy a place of their own.

Then, at noon, Brian had come home early from his teaching job at the local college and announced that he'd quit. Hated teaching, he'd said, couldn't stand it anymore. Was changing his life. Oh, and by the way, sorry, he loved her, but he was leaving her.

"What!"

"I've come to a watershed moment in my life."

"You've come to a watershed moment in your life," Stella echoed, thinking to herself that he wasn't the only one who was a bit fed up, let alone having a watershed moment.

Brian didn't seem to notice that Stella was home from work much earlier than she should have been.

"I'm going to be a barmaid. And I'm changing my name to Doris," he blurted out.

It was then that Stella entered her not-thinking zone as she listened to Brian explain his unhappiness, which had recently started to lift when he'd met Nigel. It had been love at first sight.

Wait a minute. That's what you said to me once. Stella's mental pendulum swung back into the thinking zone and kept going all the way to memory as Brian kept talking.

Months before, they'd gone for a Sunday afternoon hike across the Downs, stopping off midway for a drink at *The Shepherd and Dog,* a fifteenth-century country pub in the fold of the hills. It's charming, they'd agreed, making their way across the sloping floor to a small table by the enormous fireplace blackened by centuries of use which extended to the side walls giving the room a dimmed and slightly sooty, yet somehow comforting patina. It was popular too, Stella noticed, eying the noisy crowd as well as the low-beamed ceiling. Anyone over 5'9 had to stoop to get to their seat, if they could find one.

Brian had taken a long time ordering his pint of *Spitfire* ale and her half-pint of lager and lime, chatting away to a good-looking man behind the bar who'd turned out to be the owner, Nigel.

Brian was still talking as Stella's pendulum drifted back towards the no-thinking zone in the present. A tear slid down her cheek.

"Look Stel, I know how this must feel. We'll talk about things some more, divvy up the furniture and all that. But right now, I think I should leave."

And he had. Fast. Leaving her staring out the window. *No, he did not know how this must feel.*

The phone rang. She automatically reached for it. "Hello." There was a crackling on the line then it cleared.

"Stella, Auntie Barb, dear, calling from America to wish you a Happy Birthday."

"I'm not twenty-nine until tomorrow."

"Oh, well, blame it on the time difference. What are your plans? Brian taking you somewhere nice for dinner?"

"Brian just left me for his new boyfriend." Stella was still trying to wrap her mind around this latest bit of bad news. Why hadn't she realized ... something? She'd thought nothing of it when he'd slipped on a pair of her silk panties once and remarked, "Omigod, these feel fantastic next to my skin!" putting it down to just a bit of foreplay, one of their sex games.

"I'm so sorry for you dear. Break-ups are never easy; he has lousy timing. And a he, not a she!" Aunt Barbara sighed. "Well, it is 1993. *And the times they are a chan-gin,*" she sang. Auntie Barb was fond of Bob Dylan, the Rolling Stones, too. Almost any musician, since she'd followed one to America decades ago in her youth.

Stella didn't want to think or talk about Brian any more.

"Where are you living now, Auntie?"

"Still in California. I bought an old apartment building at the beach. Venice."

Theirs had never been a close-knit family, Stella reflected. Auntie Barb had stayed in touch intermittently, occasionally sending a Christmas card with her current address and a couple of lines about her life. She'd never been back to England, and no one in the family had ever gone to America to visit. Her musician husband, Ray, had died a few years ago.

Stella turned back to look out of the window. "That sounds very nice Auntie."

"Oh, it is. Lovely weather, in the seventies. Sunny. A breeze off the ocean that keeps the air nice and fresh. You should come and visit me sometime. I've got an extra Murphy bed."

Stella didn't know what a Murphy bed was, but the offer sounded tempting. She could do with a holiday right now, somewhere far, far away. They chatted for a few more minutes and then Aunt Barb said she had to sign off. It was time to go surfing with the neighbors.

Surfing? Aunt Barb must be about fifty now. Wasn't she a bit past—surfing?

"Happy Birthday again, dear. Do something nice for yourself even if it is without Brian. Life is short."

CHAPTER 2

Stella staggered out of LAX at 11:30 p.m. the following evening. It had been a long journey–a very long journey. She'd had to change planes three times because she'd left the UK in such a hurry. After hanging up from Aunt Barbara's transatlantic call, Stella had retrieved her passport from the dresser drawer, her suitcase from the top of the wardrobe, thrown some clothes in it, and caught the bus to Gatwick Airport without much thought at all. Screw Brian. He could deal with the furniture and everything else. She was having her own watershed moment. It was entitled "Escape."

At the airport, after visiting the ATM to empty their joint bank account, Stella had dug back down in her handbag for her credit card and bought a ticket for the first transatlantic flight out, which happened to be to Chicago. The last non-stop flight to Los Angeles had already left for the day and she didn't want to wait until tomorrow for the next one. She wanted to exit NOW. Always a model of good behavior since childhood, it was the first reckless thing Stella had ever done. It didn't feel bad at all, Stella reflected. In fact, if she thought about it for half a second, it felt darn good.

Stella had tried calling her aunt back, but Barbara didn't answer the phone or have an answering machine.

From Chicago the only seat available was on a flight to Miami, and from there she'd gone onto Dallas, each time trying Auntie Barb's number to no avail. Flying across America she'd had more than a few cocktails, but also managed a few hours of sleep. It wasn't the perfect way to spend her birthday, but under the circumstances it was good enough.

Finally, I'm here. Stella's nose twitched at the burning smell of jet fumes trapped under a blanket of fog as she stepped out of the airport and into the Los Angeles night. She tried calling her aunt again, but no luck. She hailed a taxi.

"Los Angeles is a very large city," her aunt had once told her. "And very spread out. It takes ages to get around. The traffic's horrendous, and public transportation only slightly above nil."

Stella was more than mildly surprised when the cab glided to a stop at a dead-end street twenty minutes later. The ride hadn't taken "ages" at all.

"Ocean Front Walk, commonly known as the Boardwalk," the driver announced, turning the meter off. "The address you want is just along to your right, next to this building." He indicated a shuttered corner grocery store.

"Are you sure?" Stella got out of the Yellow Cab and surveyed her surroundings. She was standing on a curb, a wide strip of asphalt in front of her giving way to sand that quickly faded into blackness. The sighing of the sea could be heard washing onto the shore beyond that. It was after midnight and there wasn't another soul around.

"Yep."

The cabbie took her money, made a U-turn, and drove off leaving Stella standing under a tall skinny palm tree glowing neon-green in the fuzzy half-light from a street lamp. She shivered. It wasn't cold, just damp from swathes of fog encircling everything. And apart from the sound of the ocean out there in the dark it was very, very quiet. Stella felt a frisson of panic. Maybe she shouldn't have acted so hastily after all. Too late now.

The Boardwalk was empty as Stella wheeled her suitcase along until she came to a white picket fence with a gate in it. *Was this it?* She couldn't tell. The stucco building across the concreted yard looked old and more like a house than an apartment building. All the windows were in darkness. Stella took a deep breath, opened the creaking gate and walked up the stone steps to the front door, which had *Billy's* written in faded gilt paint across the glass panel. Yes, she seemed to be in the right place according to what Auntie Barb had mentioned.

She hated to wake her aunt up, but it couldn't be helped. Stella turned on her keychain light and searched for a doorbell. There wasn't one. She tried the doorknob. It was loose, but the door opened onto a small hallway directly in front of her with a flight of stairs going up to the second floor. She stepped inside and flashed her light around looking for a light switch, but there didn't seem to be one of those, either. A door to her left had number "1" on it. The door to her right said number "2." There were eight apartment mailboxes along one wall. Stella looked for her aunt's name and saw it written in black marker on number "8." The two doors at the top of the stairs were numbered "3" and "4."

"Where the hell is number 8," she said out loud to herself, starting to feel tired and grouchy.

"Round the back, across the courtyard," answered a young woman's voice entering the front door behind Stella, making her jump.

"Didn't mean to scare you." The young woman wore black pants, a black t-shirt with a Venice restaurant's name scrawled across the front of it and a food-splashed apron slung over one shoulder. She inserted a key into door number 2 and flipped on a light switch that shined out from the apartment and into the hall. "Who're you looking for?"

"Barbara Smith."

There was a moment's silence as the woman, who was about her age and pretty in a cinematic way with brown hair and tired eyes, stared at Stella and her suitcase.

"She's my aunt," Stella explained.

"Go out the front door, down the steps and turn left. You'll come to a path leading between this building and the grocery next door. Follow it through to the courtyard and the building at the back, which has an outside wooden staircase leading up to apartments 7 and 8. Number 8 is the first one at the top of the stairs."

"Thank you," Stella said, opening the door and stepping out.

"Be careful. It's very dark back there." The door to number 2 closed behind her.

She found the path. It was narrow and almost pitch black as the grocery next door was built right up to the property line forming a roofless tunnel between the neighboring buildings. Her footsteps echoed down the concrete path as she carefully made her way along. Suddenly, it opened up onto a courtyard and garden with trees and bushes in heavy shadows under the fog-laden sky. Stella didn't notice the fluffy white cat sitting on the edge of an elevated pond as she passed by until it hissed loudly and growled, startling her in the quietness and causing her to almost trip over a possum lumbering towards a flagstone patio. Stella quelled any panicky thought about what other nightlife might be lurking in the bushes, and quickly looked for the wooden stairs. Her keychain light was fading.

As she placed her foot on the first step, Stella trod on something and almost tripped again. The last ray of light shone from the keychain for a second, then abruptly died as she screamed. It wasn't another animal; it was a dead body.

Decorative loops of white Christmas lights snapped on in the covered back porch above her head, and a door opened.

"Who's there? What's going on?"

Stella looked up to see a gray-haired woman peering over the balcony railing that had several bathing suits and towels hung over the ledge to dry.

"Aunt Barbara?" Stella squeaked.

"Just a minute." The woman reached back into her kitchen for a flashlight, then shone a bright light down where Stella stood, quaking. "Christ!" She quickly walked along the porch and came halfway down the stairs, making her way among some overturned potted plants, then stopped.

"I'm not Barbara." Her flashlight shone down on the body. "She is."

CHAPTER 3

Stella spent the next few hours sitting in a garden chair on the patio answering questions from the police, who'd arrived at the same time as the paramedics. The gray-haired neighbor who'd introduced herself as Carol sat next to her. Carol told an officer that she'd arrived home from her landscape gardening job about 8:00 p.m. tired out, her back aching, after stopping off *en route* at the plant nursery and the supermarket.

"I had a bath, a bite to eat, took two Extra Strength Excedrin, and fell asleep watching television. I didn't see Barbara or anyone else this evening and didn't hear anything unusual until this woman's scream woke me."

Carol had switched on more Christmas lights that were strung across the patio on bamboo poles between the trees. The fog tinged everything with fuzzy edges. A soft breeze coming off the ocean stirred the lights, making them gently dance like a flock of fireflies under a canopy of purple bougainvillea above the patio.

I feel as if I'm in a dream Stella thought. But this wasn't any dream. It was a nightmare. She felt tired, yet wide awake at the same time. Auntie Barb was *dead*? How could this be happening? She'd sounded so cheerful on the phone yesterday; a ray of sunshine in the sudden sinkhole of Stella's life. Visiting her aunt had seemed like a lovely momentary escape, a time out. Instead, Stella felt she was sinking even further. She swore she could see several pairs of gleaming eyes hidden in the bushes.

"Cats," Carol said, noticing them, too. "Several tenants have one. They hang out with the possums after dark. Your aunt's cat is named Mr. Velvet. He's probably out on the beach right now stalking sleeping seagulls. She loved that cat." Carol glanced at Stella for a beat after wiping tears from the corner of her eyes. "You know, you look a lot like Barbara, although her hair was long and brown, not short and black. Same green eyes. Do they run in the family?"

"My mother told me we both had her mother's eyes," Stella replied, stifling her own tears.

"That figures."

The young woman from the front building, who introduced herself as Liz, had come out to join them in her robe and pajamas after the police had knocked on her door. The tenant who lived above her in apartment 4 was currently staying in Manhattan Beach with her boyfriend. The occupant of number 1 wasn't home, either, and neither was Greg, the tenant in apartment 3, According to Carol, Greg owned some land out near Frazier Park off the 5 freeway across from the Los Angeles Astronomy Society.

"He's probably out there stargazing," she added. "It wouldn't be foggy in the mountains."

"Looks like Sam and Andrea aren't around, either," Liz sighed looking towards apartments 5 and 6 directly under Carol and Barbara's apartments. "Oh, this is just awful. Poor

Barbara," she sniffled, retrieving a wrinkled Kleenex from a pocket in her robe.

"I just can't believe it. Barbara was so full of life, and now she's gone." Carol wiped her eyes again.

The police were conferring with the paramedics and personnel from the Coroner's office. They'd examined the stairs and Aunt Barbara, even gone into her apartment briefly since the door was already ajar.

The sergeant who'd taken Stella's statement came over and sat down next to her. "It looks like your aunt stepped out onto the porch sometime late this evening to water her potted plants, tripped and fell. We found a spilled watering can near the top of the stairs. Those steps are in bad shape, too. They need replacing before someone else has an accident and breaks their neck."

"Greg in apartment 3's supposed to fix them," Carol responded, clearing her throat. "He just rebuilt the front building's back stairs, but hasn't gotten round to these yet." She jerked her head towards the rear apartments.

"I'd advise him to do it sooner rather than later before someone else breaks a leg. Or worse." The sergeant, whose LAPD patch said "Pacific Division," nodded towards Aunt Barb's body as he turned to Stella. "Are you the next of kin?"

I dunno, Stella thought dejectedly. *Am I?* She was having a hard time processing this latest event, and felt too tired to cry. "Barbara was my aunt, my mother's sister. I'm her niece, her only niece. She didn't have any children." An unbidden thought crept into her mind. *A far as I know.*

The sergeant nodded. "Okay, close enough. You're it. Your aunt's death seems to have been an accident, but since there weren't any witnesses they'll take her body downtown to the coroner's office where she'll be examined further. If there's no need for an autopsy, the medical examiner will sign off on the death certificate. Someone will call you after that and see which funeral home you want her released to." He handed her his business card with the name "Martinez" and the station phone number on it and went back to the accident scene.

Stella blinked. Loss of her job had been bad enough, let alone loss of her home, loss of her boyfriend, a hellacious birthday journey to this improbable paradise, discovering her dead relative before they'd even met, and now *a funeral?*

She stood silently with Carol and Liz as they watched the coroner's team load the stretcher with Aunt Barb into their unmarked black van parked beside the paramedics and police car parked on the service road that ran parallel to the Boardwalk. A tear ran down Stella's cheek as the Coroner's van drove away and the others followed, their tail lights disappearing into the night as they turned left onto Brooks Avenue. *Poor Aunt Barb. Now we'll never get to know each other!*

"Barbara was a great lady, just great," Liz said sadly, yawning and turning to walk back to her own apartment. "Sorry, I have to get some sleep. I have an audition for a commercial first thing in the morning. Goodnight."

"Goodnight," Stella and Carol muttered automatically.

"Hope Liz gets the job; she needs a break." Carol said. "Barbara was my friend as well as my landlady. Oh, this is all too terrible. What an awful introduction to America this is for you, too."

Stella didn't know what to say. Her mother would have advised her to check her horoscope before dashing off on such a long journey. Precisely why she hadn't called her. *Now I'll have to phone Mum and let her know her sister's dead.* Sheila was currently holidaying in Spain with her second husband, Jim. Stella sighed wearily and tilted her head back to look up at the night sky. No moon in sight. *That's because it's in ca-ca.*

CHAPTER 4

Carol pointed back towards the apartment building, "You can access your aunt's place by her front door." The two buildings were the exact same style, standing back-to-back but separated by the courtyard garden. One building faced the Boardwalk, the other faced the service road, ironically called Speedway, with a posted speed limit of 10 miles per hour. Carol led Stella upstairs and showed her where Auntie Barb hid number 8's front door key.

"The cops left your back door open. Remember to close it." Carol opened her own front door, hesitated, then thought better of it. "Sorry, but I'm too exhausted to talk more right now. It'll be dawn in a couple of hours. I have to get some sleep. Goodnight."

After fumbling for the light switch Stella stood in a dining-room with a table and chairs set in front of a window. She tried not to feel like an intruder in her aunt's home but what could else could she do in the middle of the night? Not to mention being short of funds for a hotel. To her left was a built-in wall credenza with two doors on either side, one leading to a bathroom and the other to the kitchen. To her right a doorway led into a back room which served as a living room as well as her aunt's bedroom.

Carol had said, "Your aunt has a Murphy bed. Just pull the handle on the wall to bring it down."

Stella picked up her suitcase and walked into the bedroom cum living room containing a couch and television, plus a desk. A head-high shelf covered in books ran around the walls interrupted by a window with closed blinds on the far wall, a closet door to her left and the Murphy bed handle to her right. She pulled it and a double-sized bed descended with fluffy blankets and soft pillows.

"Aaaahhh." It looked so comfortable and inviting that Stella kicked off her shoes, closed her eyes and was about to sink onto it before she remembered the back door was still open. Reluctantly, she padded through the shotgun apartment in her bare feet and into the small kitchen.

Carol had already turned off the Christmas lights on the porch and down on the patio. Darkness entrenched everything. Stella could hear the ocean out there heaving and swelling in the damp night air. As she went to pull the back door closed a gauzy swathe of fog parted and a ribbon of moonlight shone across the dark sea. For a moment Stella caught the faint reflection of starlight on the water before gray mist closed over the moon again. But not before her eye had also caught another reflection. The moon had momentarily back-lit the shadow of someone standing behind net curtains in the house next door. And that person was watching *Billy's* apartments. And her. She shivered.

CHAPTER 5

Stella awoke to the sound of loud banging. Feeling groggy and a little bit hungover she'd fallen asleep on top of Aunt Barbara's bed still in the clothes she'd worn to the office, not bothering to change before her sudden departure and flights across America. She felt grungy. *I need a cup of tea.* She also needed to investigate where the noise was coming from.

A man in a checked flannel shirt was hammering new planks of wood into the top of the staircase. He looked up startled and not particularly friendly as Stella opened the back door,

"Who are you?"

"I'm Stella. Who are you?"

"Greg." He waved one arm in the direction of his apartment across the garden. "Barbara asked me to replace the stairs. Is she around?"

Stella vaguely remembered Carol telling the police that her aunt had hired one of the tenants to repair the back stairs. She also recalled Carol mentioning he was away, probably stargazing at the night sky from his property north of Los Angeles. *Maybe he doesn't know about the accident yet.*

"Um, no. I'm her niece."

She explained what had happened. Greg listened, then was silent for a moment. He looked down at the step he'd been replacing.

"Shit."

Stella thought that adequately summed everything up.

"Look, I'm sorry to mention this," Greg continued, not sounding very sorry at all, "but how am I going to get reimbursed now? I paid for the lumber on my credit card. They cut it to size." He gestured to a short stack of planks in the garden below. "Barbara said to just give her the bill, plus whatever my time was." He fished into his jeans pocket and held out a crumpled receipt for the wood.

He didn't appear duly unruffled about his landlady's demise, although Stella could certainly understand the part about paying his credit card bill. She glanced at the receipt, then down at the stairs. It looked pretty straightforward to her, just nail in new planks. But then she didn't know a thing about carpentry or construction.

"How long d'you estimate it'll take to fix?" She struggled to appear business-like for the sake of her aunt's memory. *God, how I wish you were here Aunt Barb; I miss you. But, how can you miss someone you've never met and only communicated with a few times?*

Greg considered. "Couple of days. I have to varnish the steps when they're finished."

"How much had you and my aunt agreed upon for your labor?" Stella wondered if there was anything written down somewhere memorializing that conversation.

Greg hesitated for a fraction of a second. "She was going to take it off the rent."

"Which would be about–how much?" Stella was now wide-awake.

"Ballpark?" Greg named a price, then added, "More if I finished ahead of time."

That didn't seem out of line from the little Stella knew about the character of her aunt. She nodded. "Okay, then I'll leave you to it."

She stepped back into the kitchen and closed the door. Fixing the steps had to be done as soon as possible so Greg may as well continue, especially since Barbara appeared to have sanctioned it. Taking the cost off of the rent didn't sound like such a bad idea on either side. Stella wouldn't be surprised if Auntie Barb had made those kind of deals all the time. It sounded like a simple way of doing things with plenty of room for creative accounting.

Her eyes lit on the kettle on top of the stove. Now, tea. Quick. She rummaged through the larder and found several different types. *Sleepytime? No, I don't think so. Red Zinger? Maybe.*

"Ahh." Stella pulled out a box of Taylor's of Harrogate off the shelf, a reliably strong black tea guaranteed to knock your socks off, then went into the bathroom after putting the kettle on to boil.

What, no shower? Just a claw-foot bath tub. And another door. Just how many entrances and exits did this place have? Auntie Barb had mentioned in their phone conversation that *Billy's* had been built as beach apartments in 1910 for weekenders and their guests escaping the inner city heat of Los

Angeles. The red car trolley had run from downtown along Venice Boulevard to the ocean in those days.

People staying in the apartment could change into their bathing costumes in the bathroom and go directly out onto the porch, down the back stairs and through the garden, exiting the front gate directly onto the Boardwalk and the sand without ever having to pass through the dining-room or kitchen. Likewise, they could directly re-enter the bathroom to change after a swim, either hanging wet swimsuits and towels over the porch rail or dumping them in the bathtub without dripping seawater on the kitchen or dining-room floors. The apartment itself was small, but Stella bet it could comfortably accommodate quite a few people running in and out to the beach on those long-ago weekends. She'd spied another handle on the dining-room wall, and another Murphy bed behind it. *That must be the other one Aunt Barb had mentioned in the phone call.*

Stella needed milk for her tea but there wasn't any in the refrigerator. Remembering the grocery store next door, she retrieved some American money from her handbag obtained from what was left on her credit card at an LAX ATM, slipped on her shoes, and headed out.

The garden seemed much friendlier in daylight, very lush and colorful with tubs of roses and other assorted flowers blooming amongst the trees and bushes. Hummingbirds hovered around the purple canopy of bougainvillea. She paused by the white picket fence before opening the gate to the Boardwalk. It was a beautiful day now that last night's fog had cleared. Palm trees rustled in the morning breeze. Stella looked past people cycling and roller-skating along the bike path across the wide expanse of white sand to the sparkling blue ocean. Were those *dolphins* surfing on the incoming tide?

All along the Boardwalk venders and shopkeepers were rolling up their shutters and laying out souvenir goods for the tourists. People jogged and walked their dogs. She watched a trio of young Asians reading and talking from a script one of them carried as they walked along while a fourth traveled backwards filming his friends with a hand-held camera. He swiveled between them to a building mural, then some wall graffiti. When they came abreast of some homeless Vets waking up on benches in the pagoda the camera was rapidly readjusted to capture close-ups of sleeping bags, unwashed faces, bloodshot eyes.

The municipal trash truck lumbered into view spewing a smell of exhaust fumes as it slowed. The camera switched to filming discarded tennis shoes and jeans emptied from a trash can. Stella looked away and opened the gate. She did not want to imagine the film makers' closeup of stale pizza crusts and Styrofoam soda cups tumbling after them.

A man wearing a reticulated python wrapped loosely around his neck and pushing a baby stroller filled with Macaw parrots walked past her and took up a place under a nearby palm tree. His female companion carried a playpen which she set down and unfolded, arranging several pink and blue crocheted blankets inside. She then set out a sign suggesting photographs could be taken for a donation if someone wanted to wear a snake or become a birdman as the guy placed the python in the playpen. He then stretched out his arms and five Macaws and one little green parrot flew out of the stroller and arranged themselves along his arms.

Definitely not Brighton seafront. Stella walked past a small pizza takeout carved out of the grocery building space and into Ocean Front Market. Her stomach rumbled as she pulled a carton of low fat milk from the refrigerator. She decided she needed breakfast to go with her cup of tea. After perusing the cereal section, she chose a box of Cheerios because the name appealed to her. Stella needed cheering up after the past few days.

She was standing in line by the cash register behind three other customers when the Snake and Parrot man came running in the open door.

"Has anyone seen my python?"

For some reason everyone, Stella included, looked down at the floor around their ankles.

"Was it the small one–or that great big adult?" Mr. Patel, the storekeeper, looked up nervously from the cash register as another shopper briefly checked out the aisles.

"The juvenile, the six-footer. There's a tiny hole in a corner of the playpen netting and somehow he managed to squeeze out."

"Wow, a reptile strolling along the Boardwalk. How novel is that?" A couple of customers snickered..

"Is he hungry?" Mr. Patel had left the cash register and was now eyeballing the stock on his shelves.

"Probably. But he could go a few days, maybe a week, tops."

An LAPD patrol car cruised slowly by on the Boardwalk. The Snake and Parrot man rushed out towards it.

"Let me know if you see Monty, okay?" he called over his shoulder.

"Oh, most definitely," Mr. Patel replied, looking around nervously as he went back to the cash register.

Stella paid for her groceries and hurried back to *Billy's.* A bare-chested man in a leather helmet came wind-surfing down the bike path as she opened the gate. His ultra tight short-shorts were cinched into a leather belt with an over-sized Harley Davidson logo buckle as he carefully balanced on one leg while clutching a big red sail.

"Hey, you! You're gonna get a ticket for speeding!" One of the LAPD patrol officers shouted as his partner, who Stella recognized as Officer Martinez from the night before, was examining the playpen and jotting down particulars from the Snake and Parrot man.

The windsurfer looked around the edge of his sail and immediately started picking up speed with both of his legs. The homeless men in the pagoda cheered him on as he disappeared around a bend in the bike path.

Never a dull moment Aunt Barb had said on the phone to Stella when describing where she lived.

"You got that right, Auntie," Stella smiled to herself as the opened the gate and strolled down the narrow concrete path between the buildings to number 8 feeling a little sad again.

As Stella sat down to breakfast at the dining-room table she noticed the dining-room window was wide open. Not her doing. *Now why didn't I notice that before.* Tree branches from a pinion pine leaning over the fence from the garden next door filled the window frame. *No need for curtains here.* A small Japanese serenity bell hung from the nearest branch tinkling gently in the late morning breeze. Stella smiled to herself. *Aunt Barb's handiwork, no doubt. Wait a minute, what's that?* A pair of green eyes blinked at her. A black cat crouched deep in the piney foliage. Suddenly, it sprang forward leaping through the open window and landing on the dining-room table. Aunt Barbara's cat door? *Bloody hell, another entrance to this place.*

"You must be Mr. Velvet," Stella addressed the feline remembering Carol's mention of the tenants' cats. Stella was partial to cats. She'd had one while growing up. Brian, however, had been allergic so she'd had to go cat-less for the past five years. *Brian. The least of my worries right now.*

Mr. Velvet sat on the table while Stella ate, keeping one eye on her and one eye on the cereal bowl as he licked his paws and gave himself a morning wash. Grooming over, he stuck his head in the bowl to lick up the milk residue as Stella drank her cup of tea.

The phone rang. It was the coroner's office. The medical examiner had examined her aunt's body, found no evidence of foul play and agreed with the interim police report. Aunt Barbara was ready for release. Where did Stella want to send her, which funeral home? And could she come in as soon as possible to sign the necessary papers first.

Stella explained her situation. The woman on the other end of the line was sympathetic, said their office didn't hand out advice or information, but she could give her a few days to make arrangements. And could she call back and let them know as soon as possible because the weekend was coming up, their busiest time since bodies started stacking up on a Friday night. Stella promised to do her best. She sighed and hung up. Time to call Mum.

Stella fished out her address book from her shoulder bag and called the number of the holiday rental in Spain. It would be evening over there,

Sheila took the news of her sister's death stoically. After a mini-moment's silence, with an almost imperceptible sob, she asked: "Was she stoned? Is that why she fell over?"

Stella felt an irrational urge to defend her aunt. Her mother had described Barbara as a hippie and the whole family always seemed unforgiving when talking about her. Perhaps it was because the woman had done what *she* wanted to do, not what was expected of her.

"She tripped and fell on unsafe steps, Mum." Stella felt tears coming on. "As next of kin on the scene, the authorities expect me to deal with everything. Can you come over? I don't know what to do."

"Sorry, darling, I can't be with you. We have a crisis of our own going on here. Jim's hurt his back snorkeling. He's having surgery first thing in the morning. You can do what needs to be done." Her mother's voice was encouraging. "You're good at coping. "

Except for the small digression of reading her astrological horoscope in the daily newspaper, Sheila was a practical woman. "I know it's a long shot, but look around the flat; perhaps Barbara left instructions. If not, I'd recommend cremation at the nearest place."

Stella felt a ray of hope. "Then I could bring her back to England with me!"

"Oh, God, no! She'd hate that. You're at the beach. Scatter her ashes over the ocean then she can wander around to her heart's content."

Stella could be practical, too. "I'm worried about funds. I don't have enough money to pay for that kind of thing."

"Barbara must have a checkbook or credit cards. Ray was never a penniless guitarist. He played backup for all those famous musicians at concerts and on their records, plus Barbara told your grandmother once that he wrote songs. Maybe there's residuals or royalties or whatever they're called. Look around. You're good at sorting things out, Stella; you'll come up with something, I know you will. Listen, sweetheart, I have to go. I'll call you back in a couple of days."

She hung up.

"Thanks, Mum," Stella said to the dial tone.

CHAPTER 6

Stella needed a bath and to change her clothes. Mr. Velvet was asleep on an old armchair in a corner of the dinng-room by the time she finished sprucing herself up. The hammering had stopped and Greg wasn't around. Stella presumed he was taking a late lunch break. She'd been thinking things through while lying in the tub with a sprinkle of Aunt Barbara's lavender oil in the water which had helped soothe her mind as well as her body. The cop had been right last night when he'd said: *You're it.* She had to take charge of the situation. That meant getting Auntie Barb buried or cremated. First, she'd have to look for any instructions or will plus her aunt's handbag and car keys, not to mention any wallet with money in it. Stella felt guilty at that last thought, but she was almost out of funds. *Aunt Barb would have understood. I hope.*

She rifled through the drawers and cupboards of the dining-room credenza. *Nada.* Not a check book or credit card in sight. Stella walked into the living-room cum bedroom and folded the Murphy bed back into the wall, latching it to leave a neat and tidy space in which to maneuver. She opened the closet door to put her suitcase away and there, next to her aunt's clothes was a four-drawer filing cabinet with a handbag resting on top. Inside, Stella found car keys (a Mercedes), check book (sizable bank balance) and a red leather wallet containing credit cards alongside a healthy amount of cash, which she dropped into her own handbag pushing aside any uncomfortable feelings about violating her aunt's privacy and feeling like a thief.

Then she opened the top drawer of the filing cabinet and saw neatly labeled personal files ("Bank statements," "Gas and Electric,") etc. The second drawer held an accounts ledger along with labeled files for each tenant and spare sets of keys in envelopes for their apartment.

For a freedom-loving hippie, as Stella's mother, Sheila, had once described her sister, Auntie Barb had a good sense of order and neatness, not to mention a certain business acumen. The folder for Greg's apartment, number 3, had a yellow Post-it stuck inside, with a ballpark figure for materials and labor along with a notation to take the final amount off of his next month's rent. Okay, that solved that problem. But where was the will, if there was one? Stella rifled through the other two drawers and found it. Actually, found two.

The first will was dated several years before and had a Post-it stuck to it that read "moot." The second will was dated, signed, notarized three weeks previously, and drawn up with a different law firm's signature. Barbara Smith had left everything to her "dear niece Stella Maris." *Whoa.* The first will had listed a company called Gabriel Charities as executor and beneficiary. The more recent will listed the law firm as executor and was signed by a Harry Bernstein, Esq. The second will also contained a pre-paid cremation plan and detailed her aunt's last wishes.

Feeling stunned at this turn of events–did she really own an apartment building now after being virtually on the brink of homelessness a few days before–Stella phoned the law firm and was put through to Mr. Bernstein.

"Hi there, Barbara. How's life down at the beach?"

"Um, this isn't Barbara. This is her niece from England."

Stella hated to dampen his cheery greeting, but she ploughed ahead recounting the recent turn of events, Once he got over the shock of her aunt's death, Mr. Bernstein became very sympathetic, offering his condolences as well as some helpful and practical advice, plus some personal reminiscences.

"Your aunt and I had the same taste in rock and roll. Last summer we enjoyed several concerts on the Santa Monica Pier including King of the Surf Guitar Dick Dale and his rockin' surf music from the early sixties and Indigo Girls from more recent times. We'd talked about going to a Rolling Stones concert next time they were in town. God, I'll miss Barbara."

His wistful tone became more subdued. "Now, don't worry about a thing. It'll be a relatively routine filing with the court but you might have to wait a year or two for probate to be completed. In the meantime, forward any bills to me. The tenants pay their rents into your aunt's account, so you don't have to worry about anything there. I'll be taking care of everything. When can you come in and see me so we can get the process started and look at the funeral arrangements she wanted? Tomorrow?" He named a time in the afternoon, and gave his address in Beverly Hills.

Stella put the phone down feeling relieved, like a burden had been lifted off her shoulders. Although her last job had been at a law firm, she hadn't worked much around wills and probate, but what Mr. Bernstein had told her didn't seem very different from how it worked in England. He'd sounded so supportive, too. Stella wondered how close he and her aunt actually had been. She'd find out soon enough.

Right now, she needed a break. After a liberal application of sunscreen from a bottle in the bathroom cabinet, she set out.

The white sand felt soft and warm under her bare feet as Stella walked across the beach, sandals dangling from one hand. Some people sat cross-legged in a circle near the water, one of them recounting his recent struggle with drugs. Stella surveyed the vast Pacific Ocean spread out before her, the biggest ocean on earth. The dolphins had moved on, and so had the research boat testing Santa Monica Bay water that she'd also noticed when going to the grocery store. Surfers in wetsuits were out in full force, sitting on their surfboards like mullahs on prayer mats as they waited for the perfect wave. To her right a tractor dragging an enormous rake worked the beach smoothing the wide swathe of sand, removing any debris. *Making it look pretty and perfect.* Stella walked in that direction at the edge of the waves towards the Santa Monica Pier

The water was surprisingly cold on her feet and ankles at first, the tide not fully in as she made her way around several piles of seaweed waiting to be reclaimed by the ocean. Something caught her eye by one clump and she bent down to examine it further, pushing aside rubbery tendrils. A tiny crab scuttled for cover. A larger crab appeared, covering the small one protectively, guiding it deeper into seaweed cover. *Aww, mum and baby?* Stella repositioned the seaweed tendrils over the spot. Animals might not have human thoughts, but everything in the universe communicates with every other living thing, and every living thing suffers pain, she realized. Perhaps she should let go of her anger towards Brian. *Not yet.*

As Stella walked on towards the pier she noticed a tourist and his two children looking at something. There were little translucent blobs scattered on the tideline.

"Jellyfish," the man explained to the two young boys. "Do you know that drifting is the most economical way to travel the waters of the world for jellyfish? It takes very little energy for them to gently pulse their bells," he pointed at a small diaphanous body with one of the children's sand shovels, "and ride the ocean currents."

"How'd they get here?" the older boy asked.

"A wave brought them."

"Where do waves come from, Dad?" the younger child wanted to know.

Dad acted out a wave with his hands. "They're born at the South Pole, fueled by the sun streaming down as they're driven across the planet by wind. Waves are full of molecules traveling in a circular motion bringing up nutrients from below."

Stella smiled to herself and walked on before Dad had to explain what molecules were. As she approached the pier she followed people jogging or walking underneath it to get to the beach beyond. She shivered. It was cold and damp and a little creepy under there with waves crashing against the reinforced wooden pilings and the smell of dried and rotting vegetation thrown up by the sea during high tides. The tractor raking the sand smooth obviously didn't venture under here.

Stella passed back into sunshine on the other side, then stopped. The beach stretched endlessly towards green and purple mountains in the distance. But jet lag was catching up with her. She sat down and watched a flock of brown pelicans in a low fly-by searching for fish in the waves below. The sun felt warm and comforting on her face and arms. Pretty soon she fell asleep.

She awoke very late in the afternoon with the sun much lower on the horizon. Pier lights were starting to come on. It might only be February but there were still plenty of tourists strolling the wooden boards alongside residents walking their dogs or enjoying the approaching twilight with their families. Some anglers were packing up their gear after a day of fishing from the end of the pier, while others were unpacking their rods and readying for a spot of night fishing.

Stella slowly jogged back along the Boardwalk to *Billy's*, had a drink of water, then walked along the back porch and knocked on Carol's kitchen door. There was something she needed to ask her.

"There's a lovely view from here," Stella remarked as Carol opened the door, a broom in her hand. She stepped out on the porch and they both stood for a moment looking out over the courtyard garden, watching the last of the sun slide into the sea. Although the front apartment building partially blocked a total panorama of the beach, either side of it afforded a clear scenario.

"To your left you have the Boardwalk and bike path stretching towards the Marina, and to your right they stretch past the Santa Monica pier towards Malibu with the Santa Monica mountains in the distance," Carol pointed out with the broom handle. "It's a million dollar view alright." She turned to go back inside. "I just finished sweeping up the sand that manages to get in here somehow. Come on in."

She led the way back through the kitchen, stopping to put the broom away. A human skeleton swayed and dangled from a hook on the back of the cupboard door as she opened it, the phalanges and metatarsals making a clacking sound against the wood that was muffled as Carol slammed the door shut. Stella stood transfixed. *Do I really want to go into this woman's apartment?*

Carol noticed the look on her face. "Oh, that's Norma. She's been with me since college. There was a fire in the biology lab and they had to throw everything out for insurance purposes. I rescued her from the trash."

"You named her?" Stella had decided this might be a fun neighborly visit after all.

"I did. Norma Bates. I used her for life drawings in an art class well as well as for anatomy and biology courses. Sometimes, I'd lay her on the floor and lay down beside her to draw. We're roughly the same height. Would you like some coffee?"

"Oh—kay, thanks."

"It's fresh-brewed." Carol poured two mugs from a coffee machine and handed Stella one. "Careful, it's very hot. Let's go and sit down."

Stella decided she'd let Carol take a sip from her mug first as she followed her into the living-room.

The apartment was identical in layout to Auntie Barb's, but without the Murphy beds and painted a light purple. Carol directed Stella to one of two high-backed Polynesian chairs in front of a small television set on a coffee table. The window behind it overlooked a sandy lot at the back of the corner grocery mart. Stella could see over its' roof to Brooks Avenue.

"I can see where the taxi dropped me off last night," she said. *Was it only last night? Seems like days ago.*

Carol glanced out of the window. "Every apartment here has some sort of view, at least for the moment. Developers have been buying properties up for the last twenty years, tearing down the original houses built in Abbot Kinney's day when this area was developed during the early 1900's, and leaving empty lots until prices rise. There's quite a few in Venice right now, but it won't stay that way for much longer. The neighborhood's changing. Gentrification creep started some time ago with new fire regulations regarding wooden buildings in the beach area. Most of the houses were built of wood and had ornate gables. *Billys* and the Edwards' house next door were stuccoed over, their wooden gables sawn off to meet code; that's why they're still standing. In the Brooks Avenue area towards Lincoln Boulevard, traditionally a Black residential neighborhood, many owners have been unable to make upgrades financially. Ownership has changed rapidly in the past decade. A realtor makes an offer; the people move out. It accelerated when the film industry started moving in, desiring a more gritty landscape experience than boring upscale Malibu. Wanting to be cool, 'with the people.'" Carol made quotation marks with her fingers.

Stella nodded. Life was rapidly changing everywhere. "Why is this place called *Billy's?*"

"Because it was owned by Bill Craven's family since the 1940's," Carol replied. "His family bought it when the area was in decline and prices were cheap. His mother had *Billy's* painted on the entrance door to the front building and told her young son, 'one day this place will be yours.' And it was–until he sold it to your aunt about two years ago."

Stella perked up. "Did they know each other before she bought it?"

"Barbara and her husband lived here just before he died. Bill Craven wanted to buy a place in Idaho and spend his retirement fishing there, so he and your aunt came to a financial agreement. She left *Billy's* painted on the door as an homage to the old guy. As Liz said, she was a cool lady."

Stella digested this latest bit of news as both women sat for a few seconds in silence.

"Any news from the coroner's office?" Carol asked.

"Yes. They concur with the police and are ready to release her body."

Carol opened her mouth to say something, but was interrupted by the sound of a shouting match outside. She got up from her chair and walked through to her bedroom to look out of the window overlooking Speedway. Stella followed. Peering out into the deep twilight she saw an empty lot across the service road with a haphazard line of cars parked on it. The lot ran from Brooks Avenue on the south end to an alley that T-boned into the service road just a few yards to their left on the north end. A street lamp on the corner of the alley and Speedway cast a dim light over two elderly women fighting by the garage at the back of a large Victorian house painted yellow with green gables.

"NO! THERE! PUT IT THERE!" one of them screamed.

"QUIT POKING ME WITH YOUR WALKING STICK!" The other one shouted back at her.

"Oh, it's Vi and Edna putting out their trash cans," Carol said. "They live in that house on the corner. They come out once a week after the sun goes down, but you'll probably never meet them."

"Why not?" Stella watched the two old women wrestling with the trash cans as well as each other.

"Because they're albinos."

"Albinos?" That didn't seem a good enough reason to Stella.

"And because they hate young women. Anyone under forty. In their youth they were in a carnival show here in Venice," Carol added. "Both are in their nineties now."

"A hard and difficult life, then. In those days," Stella reasoned.

"I'm sure. But they're nasty," Carol said. "Really nasty. Gary Edwards, who lives in the house next door–your dining room window overlooks the Edwards' garden–thinks they're rather sweet when you get to know them. But he's a man. Your aunt made the mistake of saying hello to them once. After their rude response she never spoke to them again."

"I S-A-I-D P-U-T I-T T-H-E-R-E!

The one with the walking stick whacked her sister. Stella looked on in shock. *Talk about the frustration of the elderly.*

"YOU BITCH! I'LL KILL YOU!"

"Told you they were nasty." Carol turned to walk back into her living room.

"Maybe they're ill; maybe they have dementia or something." Stella had trouble believing that old women could be so violent.

"They're not sweet old ladies that's for sure," Carol replied as she and Stella sat down again.

"I've found car keys. Do you know where my aunt's car is?" Stella remembered why she'd knocked on Carol's door.

"Her old silver Mercedes is on that empty lot by the youth hostel directly across from us on the other side of the service road. My Toyota truck's parked next to it."

Stella nodded. She'd check it out in the morning. It would be daunting, but she'd have to face the LA freeways and drive downtown to the coroner's office. There was also the appointment with Mr. Bernstein. Meanwhile, she was starting to feel light-headed and realized she hadn't eaten for several hours. There hadn't been much in Auntie Barb's refrigerator, but Stella recalled the freezer being stuffed with packages of frozen chicken and steaks, as well as a pizza, which would not need defrosting. She got up to leave and thanked Carol for the coffee and the information.

"Any time," Carol replied, waiting until Stella was safely inside her aunt's apartment before closing her back door and turning off the porch lights.

Mr. Velvet sat patiently waiting next to an empty dish by the stove as Stella entered the kitchen. He stared at her pointedly as she retrieved the pizza from the freezer and switched the oven on.

"You won't be able to share my meal this time," she told him, rummaging in the pantry and finding a solitary can of cat food.

He gobbled it down while she waited for the pizza to cook. *I'll need to find a supermarket tomorrow.* Her aunt's vegetable bin was empty aside from some sad-looking lettuce leaves. Stella had noted that Mr. Patel's grocery next door carried only a basket of apples and oranges on the counter, not fresh produce.

She carried her pizza into the living room cum bedroom and sat down on the small settee to watch television as she ate, nodding off after finishing a second slice. Some hours later she woke up, turned off the television and pulled the Murphy bed down before going into the bathroom to brush her teeth. Switching off all the lights and making sure the back door was locked, Stella padded back through the dining-room on bare feet. Glancing towards the open window, she paused, then quietly moved to one side and peered down through the pine tree's branches stretching ghostly against the night sky.

It was a cloudless night and the moon was almost full, casting shadows over everything. A human silhouette stood by a darkened corner of the garage next door. Was this the guy that lived there, the one staring out at her from inside his house last night? Stella kept still for a few minutes watching, and waiting. The house next door was all dark windows, no one looking out tonight. The shadow began to move very, very slowly. *Walk out into the yard so I can see you more clearly in the moonlight.* The shadow stopped, then started moving in her direction. *No, don't. I've changed my mind.* Her heart beat fast. It couldn't be, surely. *Is that body headless?*

CHAPTER 7

The silhouette moved again, a slither of moonlight catching a sleeve. Stella felt mesmerized and immobilized at the same time, wanting to flee and hide on one hand, yet straining for a better look on the other. Her mind settled for reality. And with it came relief. This wasn't a human being after all, just a surfer's wetsuit hung up to dry and swaying gently in the night breeze! *I've got to relax more.* She walked into the bedroom where Mr. Velvet was asleep at the foot of the bed and climbed in under the covers. *After all, this is the beach.*

Loud bird noises awakened her. They came from outside and didn't sound like seagulls. Stella got out of bed and walked over to the window. She opened the blinds looking out onto Speedway. Sunshine was beginning to thin a light fog which had descended during the night. An old Mercedes was parked haphazardly amongst other vehicles on the empty lot across from her window. Auntie Barb's car. A broken chain surrounding the lot had a *No Parking* sign mangled in the dirt.

Another strange bird-like squawk erupted from a cyclist pedaling down the alley towards her. Suddenly, loud chirping cries emanated from the apartment below; a call and response duet filled the air. The cyclist pulled alongside *Billy's*. A door slammed. Stella watched a woman's blonde head emerge from the building and approach the cyclist, still chirping. The two broke off the cacophony for a kiss, then the young woman lifted her long white skirt in imitation of a can-can move–revealing a significant lack of underwear–before climbing onto the back of the bicycle.

The two lovebirds rode off into the morning mist, turning left at Brooks Avenue like the coroner's van had done two nights before.

Stella couldn't wait to meet the rest of Aunt Barb's tenants. She folded the bed back into the wall leaving a neat and tidy space of living-room. Mr. Velvet was nowhere in sight. Stella put the kettle on to boil. Outside on the back porch, Greg was varnishing the wooden steps he'd hammered into place the day before. She decided not to interrupt him; he'd give her the bill soon enough. First things first: a cup of tea.

Stella consulted the *Thomas Guidebook to Los Angeles* she'd found in one of the credenza drawers and mapped out her route to the coroner's office downtown while she ate breakfast. The freeways looked daunting. She told herself the traffic couldn't be any worse than London or Paris, then gathered her shoulder bag, her aunt's car keys, retrieved the latest will with Mr. Bernstein's signature on it from the filing cabinet and set out, locking the front door firmly behind her.

"Hello," a voice called as she was about to cross Speedway to the parking lot.

Stella glanced over to where a middle-aged man wearing a white surgeon's coat and an old cotton beach hat stood inside the garage next door running his white cotton-gloved hands over two broken surfboards laid out side by side on trestles. A painter's nose and mouth mask rested below his chin and a pair of acrylic goggles was pushed up to his hat brim

"I'm really sorry about your aunt. Liz told me what happened. I'm Gary Edwards by the way."

The nosy neighbor next door. He seemed friendly enough in daylight. Stella noticed the wetsuit had been taken down. She walked over and introduced herself. Her nose twitched. "Why do I smell coconut?"

"It's the surf wax," Gary replied, indicating another surfboard propped against the garage wall. He picked up what looked like a bar of soap from his work bench and held it out towards her. "Smells so good they have to put a warning on it."

DO NOT EAT was written on the side of the bar.

"There's different types for different water and they all have a different smell. Santa Monica Bay's cool water. The tropical water stuff smells different." Gary threw the surf wax back on his work bench.

"And now, I'm about to make a new paddle board from some tattered surfboards I found on the beach."

He pulled out a metal tape measure from his surgeon's coat pocket and carefully started measuring both boards on the trestles, making pencil notes on the back of an old Tides Chart booklet.

"I see," Stella nodded. "Well, nice meeting you. Goodbye." She walked back and climbed into the old Mercedes. Mercifully, it started up without any trouble. As she pulled out onto Speedway, through the rear-view mirror she saw Gary pull down his goggles, pull up his mask, then rev up a chainsaw, ready to cut off the jagged and broken parts of both surfboards.

Such interesting neighbors. Glancing towards the yellow house with the green gables where the aged sisters lived, she didn't know if that was a good thing or a bad thing.

CHAPTER 8

The Medical Examiner-Coroner's office was a small building on the sprawling grounds of the Los Angeles County Hospital and University of Southern California Medical Center. As Stella entered the lobby, she saw a family clustered in a corner sobbing on each other's shoulders. A receptionist informed her there would be a short wait. Perhaps she'd like to visit the gift shop? *Gift shop?* Stella followed the receptionist's finger pointing towards a discreetly marked closed door. *Oh–kay.*

"Welcome to *Skeletons in the Closet!*" a woman by the cash register chirped as Stella entered a room that was approximately the size and shape of a large walk-in cupboard. She checked the back of the door as she closed it to make sure there wasn't a relative to Carol's Norma hanging there.

A display of toe-tag key rings, sweat shirts and beach towels imprinted with a dead body outline, and a rack of barbecue aprons with *"LA Coroner has heart, spare hands and spare ribs"* lettering and images confronted her when she turned back to the small space.

Really, the American penchant for chasing the almighty dollar was too much. Surely the coroner's office as a county institution didn't have to fund itself?

"Whose idea was this?" she asked the middle-aged cashier.

"A few of the medical examiners thought it up."

Amazing what doctors think about while their hands are inside someone's entrails.

"All proceeds go to at-risk youth programs," the cashier informed her. "Especially to do with drunk driving."

"Ah, good cause." Stella spied an inexpensive glass votive candle holder with the dead body imprint on one side and "Los Angeles County Coroner" written on the other side. Since Stella believed in contributing to worthy causes, she bought it. *I'm going to light a candle for you, Aunt Barb.*

"This makes a lovely little souvenir," the cashier commented wrapping up the glass in a page from the *Los Angeles Times*. I guess you could also use it as a juice glass."

No, I don't think so.

It didn't take long to sign the necessary paperwork. Although the coroner's office didn't dispense advice they were helpful in answering any of Stella's questions and gave her driving directions to the funeral home Auntie Barb had chosen.

The funeral home's staff were equally helpful. Stella signed their paperwork then walked out into Los Angele smog-hazy sunshine considering that she'd done the hardest part except for collecting the ashes. Barbara had left explicit instructions in her will for how those were to be dispersed. It struck Stella how odd it was that her aunt had been so detailed in her last wishes. *Perhaps she had a premonition.*

Part of her felt very sad as she walked to the car, which was parked outside an art gallery. She consulted her watch. It was still too early for her appointment with Mr. Bernstein. It was also about ten degrees hotter Downtown than at the beach, the air more humid. The gallery was open. She decided to go in and look around for a while.

An artist was in the middle of hanging some of her artwork inside. The woman moved back a few paces after placing her last painting.

"Oh, pardon me," she said, inadvertently bumping into Stella. "My opening's next week and I'm lost in thought with all the details. What do you think of this one?" She indicated one of the paintings.

"I really don't know anything much about art," Stella replied contemplating the abstract slashes of bright and dark colors on the canvas. It looked like chaos to her.

"I'm trying to depict the image of women in business suits and their secret dreams of hidden interior lives."

"Ah." *Trying to figure that out could give a person a headache.*

"I think I succeeded in this one, don't you?"

I can't say it looks like one big mess, can I? Stella aimed for a positive note. "I think so."

The artist turned to her, beaming. "I'm Olivia Rodriguez. Where's your accent from?"

"The UK."

Olivia smiled. "I've been to London. I really enjoyed the Tate Gallery."

Stella nodded. "I went there once on a school trip."

"I was about to take a break. Want some coffee?" Olivia walked over to a desk and held up a stainless-steel carafe

Stella felt she needed a pick-me-up; her energy was flagging. "That would be lovely."

They sat by the desk, drinking coffee and chit-chatting. Olivia did most of the talking, mainly about art at first, but then it turned out they'd both had recent breakups with lovers. By the time she left the gallery, Stella felt she'd held her own.

After saying she'd try to attend the art opening, and getting driving directions from Downtown to the law office, Stella waved goodbye and left Olivia contemplating her artwork again. She felt so good that after pulling away from the curb she almost made a left turn onto the wrong side of the road. A man leaned out of his car window and gave her the middle finger.

"Stupid women drivers!" he screamed.

Got to pay more attention.

Mr. Bernstein, the lawyer, was an affable middle-aged man who greeted Stella with a warm smile which put her at ease. He shook her hand, offered his condolences once again and directed her to a chair in front of his desk. She hadn't known what to expect and was rather surprised at his appearance, which she surmised as Beverly Hills casual: a lightweight wool sweater over an open-necked white shirt and gray slacks. Obviously not a courtroom day for him. Everyone had worn a suit to work, court appearance that day or not, at her previous law office job in England. This was a different time and place she reasoned settling into the chair. At least people behaved in a familiar, normal manner here. Mr. Bernstein had even offered her a cup of tea with milk or lemon.

"We have quite a few British clients," he explained.

Olivia's coffee had fortified her, but Stella needed a bit more of a pick-me-up to keep her going until she got back to the apartment. Jet lag was creeping up again.

She and Mr. Bernstein agreed on which were her responsibilities and which details he would take care of regarding Aunt Barbara's wishes as stipulated in the will.

"Your aunt deposited enough money in her client account to take care of legal expenses for a while," the attorney informed her.

"Why, what else did she want done?" Stella was curious.

"I don't know. We hadn't gotten around to that," Mr. Bernstein said ruefully. "Our law firm just billed her for the will so far. The up-front deposit only applies to new clients the firm takes on. We found it necessary to implement that rule after some of our more famous clients took their time paying up."

Stella nodded. She'd noticed that at her old law firm; the wealthier the client was, the longer they took to pay their bills. Often this was because an accountant or business manager was in charge of their finances.

"One thing I'm curious about Mr. Bernstein."

"Yes?"

"My aunt had a previous will which was different to the current one that she had you draw up. This latest one," Stella indicated Aunt Barb's will that Mr. Bernstein had had his secretary retrieve from the files and now lay on his desk, "is very detailed regarding what type of funeral she wanted. I mean, she wasn't *that* old."

"True. Most people don't have an exact plan in place regarding their funeral wishes until they're much older. And too many people put off making a will at all thinking they're going to somehow live forever. But remember, your aunt had property so she wanted to protect that. As regards her funeral plans, I can't comment except to say that Barbara was what I would call a thoughtful and rather tidy person in her own way." He shrugged.

"Your aunt said she wanted to be as thorough as she could, not leave any loose ends, take care of everything at the same time so she didn't have to think about it. I thought that was very sensible. Barbara knew her wishes could be amended later."

"And," Mr. Bernstein leaned back in his chair. "I seem to remember she mentioned there'd been some problem after her husband died and she didn't want a repeat of anything like that."

Stella didn't remember her mother or grandmother gossiping about any problems. Their attitude had always been that Barbara was the problem. Full stop.

"My aunt usually sent a Christmas card to the family every year with a few lines mostly letting us know if she'd changed her address. We knew she'd married Ray at one point, but she never mentioned any problems after he died."

Mr. Bernstein nodded. "She didn't say what it was and I got the idea it wasn't relevant anymore."

"Now," he sat forward. "You mentioned you were here on vacation. How long are you staying?"

"I don't know. Long enough for the funeral. After that..." she trailed off. "I have no idea what comes next in my life."

Mr. Bernstein reminded Stella of her late father sans the glasses. She found herself giving him a brief run-down of what had made her decide to take up her aunt's offer of a "vacation."

The lawyer nodded sympathetically. "You've been blind-sided by events. Take it easy for a while. You can live in the apartment rent-free since you're already an occupant and your aunt invited you to stay there. When you go back to England it can be rented out. Just send me the utility bills and they'll be paid out of the estate, as well as other bills. You can't use her credit cards or withdraw money from her bank account, however."

Stella thought about the money in her aunt's wallet which now resided in her shoulder bag. Did she have to declare that to the lawyer? How would she pay for food in the meantime? And fuel for the car? She'd been so stunned by reading Auntie Barb had left her everything, she hadn't absorbed all the details.

"What about cat food? What should I do about Mr. Velvet?"

Mr. Bernstein smiled. "I know how much Barbara loved that animal. If she had any money in her purse, I'm sure she'd want him fed. Look, take your time over all of this." He glanced at the will. "Your aunt stipulated that '$5,000 cash be released to my niece, Stella Maris, for immediate expenses she might incur,'" he read out loud. "That should tide you over for a bit."

"How do I access that?"

Mr. Bernstein knew the manager where her aunt banked and called him to arrange for Stella to get the cash.

"You have time to go over there before they close and sign any necessary documents." He pointed out the window across Wilshire Boulevard. "It's just across the street. Our firm banks there. I'll make a copy of the will you can show him. You hang on to your own copy."

They briefly discussed what to do about *Billy's.* Mr. Bernstein advised that she should take her time, think things over, not rush into anything. His firm could handle things if

Stella went back to England before making up her mind either to sell the apartment building or hire a property management firm to run it. "As I already mentioned, the tenants pay their rents directly into her account, so you won't have to bother with that. Any problem, refer them to me. But remember, every time I have to make a phone call or do something it's charged against the estate. Some things you can do yourself to keep costs down."

He gave her an idea of what those things could be as well as his firm's charges. Stella deemed it not unreasonable. Good legal services cost about the same in England. Besides, it was Aunt Barb's money and she had chosen this lawyer.

She left the law offices feeling like a weight had been taken off of her shoulders. Mr. Bernstein had promised to expedite things as much as he could. What had been heartbreaking disappointments compounded by insurmountable challenges just a few days ago were working themselves out–at least on the American end. Maybe she could enjoy a vacation while she was here after all, in spite of seeing to a funeral. It was fortunate Aunt Barb had been specific in her arrangements. Stella blew her a mental kiss.

By the time she had finished conducting business at the bank and carefully navigating the long crawl of evening commuter traffic back to Venice, Stella felt like she'd done a good day's work, if not two or three, and was very tired. But she still had to get groceries.

Carol had told her where the nearest supermarket was. Stella exited the Santa Monica freeway at Lincoln Boulevard taking it south before turning into *Lucky's Supermarket* crowded parking lot. She usually avoided supermarkets, preferring her local Sainsbury's or an individual greengrocer or bakery back home. However, she deemed *Lucky's* not so bad after surveying their large array of produce. Loading up on fresh vegetables and food for the cat all in one place had its advantages

By the time she exited the store twilight had turned into darkness. In spite of the parking lot lights, Stella had trouble spotting where she parked the Mercedes, partly because she'd entered the store through one set of double doors and exited though another. *Was it this row slightly to the right, or one over? Or the row after that?* She stood scanning cars in the vaguely-remembered direction, before turning to head over that way.

"Look out!" a woman's voice called as Stella located the car. There was a *whoosh* of air as a vehicle sped past, narrowly missing her from behind. It disappeared before she could identify the make or model.

"Thank you!" she called to the unknown person who'd saved her from a nasty accident, or worse. *That was a close one.*

Unlocking the Mercedes' trunk and placing the grocery bags inside, she felt unnerved by the incident. Her heart was thumping and she felt spaced out. It had almost seemed deliberate. First Aunt Barb's accident, and then this near miss. She slammed the trunk shut vowing to be more vigilant in spite of jet lag.

CHAPTER 9

Stella drove very carefully back to the apartment, feeling more than a little nervous as she'd almost made a left turn onto the wrong side of the road again. Trudging up the stairs she went to put her key in the lock before noticing that the front door was already slightly open. *I'm sure I locked it.* The spaced-out feeling was coming over her again. She checked to see that the spare key was in its hiding place, then slowly pushed the door open with the toe of her sandal and turned on the light. No one was there. *Relax Maris; you're just on edge,* she shrugged. The door handle was loose anyway and looked as if it hadn't been replaced since 1910. She'd have to get a new, more secure one installed, one that didn't rattle. One that stayed closed and locked.

Just then the outer door opened and Carol came up the stairs carrying her thermos flask, dirt streaks on her t-shirt and jeans.

"I see you found the grocery store." She nodded at the grocery bag in Stella's arms.

"Yeah, almost got run over in the parking lot. And my front door was ajar when I got here."

Carol leaned in for a closer look. "That happened to Barbara sometimes. She meant to replace the lock. Any word from the medical examiner?"

The two women stood on the small landing between their respective apartments while Stella brought Carol up to date on her visit to the coroner's office and funeral home.

"Things move along much faster here than in England. You're ready to bury or cremate the deceased ASAP after passing, while we Brits take more time. My uncle's funeral didn't occur until two weeks after he died."

"Huh. Guess we like to keep things moving right along. What do your relatives say?"

"Barbara was my mother's only sister, but they never got along and hadn't spoken in years." Stella sighed. "We're not a close-knit family." She went on to briefly tell Carol about the phone call to Spain and Jim's back surgery. "Mum can't help."

"Oh dear. Let me know if I can." Carol yawned as she turned to open her own front door. "I'm sorry. I don't mean to be rude. I spent all day planting shrubs and bushes in a client's garden, and all I want now is a nice hot bath and bed."

Stella nodded. "Thank you. Goodnight."

After the groceries were put away, Mr. Velvet had been fed, and a pre-cooked veggie quiche placed in the microwave to heat up, Stella changed into pajamas, then went to replace her copy of Auntie Barb's will and the other documents from the coroner's office, the funeral home and Mr. Bernstein's office in the filing cabinet. She noticed a yellow Post-it on the closet floor half-hidden beside some shoes, picked it up and read the word "moot." *How did that get*

down there? She shrugged. *Must have fallen off when I took the old will out to read.* The filing cabinet drawer wasn't fully closed, either. Stella put the current will, copies of her aunt's death certificate and the legal documents in a folder and stuck the Post-it back onto the old will. Her law office experience told her not to toss it just yet. Besides, Auntie Barb had kept it for a reason. She felt a little uneasy. Had someone been in the apartment?

The next morning loud knocking on the back door woke her. Greg had finished the steps, invited an inspection, and asked if they could come to an agreement–in alignment with her aunt's wishes–that the cost be taken off the rent?

"Just a minute." Stella stumbled sleepily into the bathroom and splashed her face with cold water before grabbing a fresh pair of jeans and a clean t-shirt.

Greg was down at the bottom of the stairs talking to Liz by the time she emerged.

"Looks good," Liz told him as Greg showed off his handiwork.

Stella had to agree. The new wooden planks felt sturdy and secure as she gingerly stepped down testing each one until she reached the bottom.

"I used a quick-drying varnish so they're all done; finished ahead of time." Greg looked expectantly at Stella who nodded affirmatively.

"Okay, we'll stick to my aunt's bargain with you." She'd explain it to Mr. Bernstein later, feeling he'd want to honor her aunt's wishes, even if it was written on a Post-it.

"You made him smile, a rare thing," Liz told her as Greg gave the women a salute and turned to walk back to his apartment.

'Just a minute." Stella noticed the plant pots stashed by a Norfolk pine tree which had lined the old steps. "What about these?"

"They're your aunt's, were your aunt's," Greg amended.

"Some of them belong to Carol," Liz said.

"Why don't you consult with her," Greg suggested. "I don't want to put them back in the wrong place. Carol gets specific over plants and the best placement for them." He walked away.

"Especially hers," Liz muttered.

It was too early in the day to get into any tenant issues. Stella was hungry.

"I'm going for a croissant and coffee at the Rose Café. Wanna join me?" Liz suggested.

That sounded better than a bowl of Cheerios and a cup of tea. Stella nodded. "Let me collect my shoulder bag."

"I have to get my bike out of the basement"

"Basement?"

Liz indicated a short flight of steps behind the Norfolk pine that lead to a narrow door. "Where we keep our bikes and surfboards. There's a lot of other old junk down there, too."

Stella quickly collected her bag and locked the back door. Liz was negotiating the basement steps with a vintage racer that had seen better days. "Do you ride a bike? Your aunt's yellow beach cruiser is down there if you do."

A smell of damp and mold from surfboards, wetsuits hanging on a clothes rack, plus several bikes and other people's long-forgotten belongings greeted Stella as she entered the dim basement. She pulled a cord hanging down from a ceiling beam and a battered fluorescent light bulb flickered on. Then off. Then on again. The concrete floor was wet from where the hot water heater had leaked. *Something else that needs fixing.* A variety of cardboard boxes with apartment numbers written on them were stacked to her left.

Beyond the concrete floor sturdy pilings holding up the building were sunk into a bank of compacted sand and stone that stretched toward a front retainer wall, creating a claustrophobic crawl space less than three feet high. Discarded suitcases and other rotting items, perhaps even from as far back as 1910, had been flung up there.

Stella wrinkled her nose. In spite of several mesh-covered vents at garden path level, some broken, which filtered in salty sea air as well as very dim daylight, the basement smelled suspiciously like a cat litter box that needed some serious cleaning.

She spied the yellow Schwinn splattered with rust patches. Stella backed it out, turning off the light with one hand and was just shutting the door, when a white cat streaked past her and up the steps, It sat down on the patio, tiny wriggling feet dangling from between its teeth.

"Ew-ww!" Liz said as together the horrified women watched the animal spit out its cache of baby mice, anchoring them with a paw, then proceeding to eat each squirming body one by one.

Stella shuddered. "Your cat?"

"No. Greg's," Liz replied. "His name is Hitler."

That fits.

The cat quickly polished off his meal, cleaning his whiskers and licking his paws, as the two women turned away, wheeling their bikes around the building before cycling off towards Rose Avenue.

As they sipped cappuccinos and consumed chocolate croissants at the cafe, Liz expressed condolences about Stella's vacation being ruined, asked her how she was, and how long she was going to stay?

"I don't know," Stella admitted. "I have to see to Auntie Barb's funeral first." She explained that the coroner's office was releasing the body to the funeral home, and there were still some arrangements to be made regarding the disposal of her aunt's ashes.

"It was a slip and fall accident then, just like the cops said?"

"It appears so."

Liz nodded sympathetically. "What'll happen to the apartment building?"

Stella shrugged. "I don't know."

She took a big bite of croissant and listened to Liz bemoan the dearth of affordable living space in the neighborhood. From what she'd briefly gleaned from the filing cabinet and her chat with Carol, Auntie Barb had been a reasonable landlady; the rents were cheap. Liz, Carol and Greg were probably on the lower socioeconomic level compared to people who were moving into the area. No wonder Liz was worried about a possible rent increase or being evicted from her apartment if *Billy's* was sold. Listening to her personal concerns about money and career, Stella certainly didn't blame her for asking some probing questions, but she couldn't provide any answers since she didn't have any yet. Besides, Stella was not one to usually confide in strangers. She didn't mention the will or anything about Mr. Bernstein. First things first. She had to see about a funeral.

"How did your audition for the commercial go, by the way?" Stella decided to change the subject.

"Not well," Liz admitted. "But I have a lead for another one, and I'm rehearsing for a showcase with a theater group in the valley."

"You sound very busy."

"Oh, I am, especially waitressing. I work all the hours I can get at the restaurant. The tips there are good, and one of the waiters just told me about a TV pilot that's casting soon." Liz chatted on about the difficulty of the acting business.

The two women parted ways outside the café. Liz said she was on her way to visit a friend.

"I'm glad you had time for breakfast," Stella said as they retrieved their bikes. "Thanks for inviting me."

"You're very welcome. It's my first day off in the last two weeks. I enjoyed talking to you, Stella."

"Likewise."

Mr. Bernstein had given Stella an address near the Marina to contact per Aunt Barbara's final funeral wishes as stipulated in her will. She slung her shoulder bag across her chest and set off for the bike path along the beach towards Venice Pier, glancing over at *Billy's* as she cycled past. It's pinkish-beige stucco walls and white woodwork took on a mellow air in the morning sunlight. It was old, but not *too* shabby, and definitely much more friendly-looking in daylight than it had been on the night she'd arrived. She shivered at the memory and pedaled faster.

A conga line of roller-skaters danced along the Boardwalk to funky music blaring out from a boombox one of them carried. Further along a pair of beach cops in their navy shorts and polo shirts were laughing and posing with some women tourists. *Instead of calling it the Pacific Division maybe they should re-christen it to the PR Division.* Stella thought of the Brighton Police; their concession to summer, when it arrived, consisted of rolling up their long shirtsleeves and exchanging their black police helmets for white ones.

When she reached Venice Pier and the bike path ended, Stella zig-zagged onto Speedway per Mr. Bernstein's instructions, cycling past Anchorage and Buccaneer Streets. The closer she got to the Marina, the newer and more upmarket the apartment buildings became. A much smaller-scale Boardwalk—more of a path with no cycling allowed and definitely no signs of commerce or hawking of beach gear–ran between the apartments and the sand.

When she came to Driftwood Street Stella found the address she was looking for at an old house on the corner. No one answered the front door, so she went around the back to where a note was tacked to the garage door: "Back Later." It seemed like a strange place for business, but nothing was beginning to surprise her any more.

Stella decided she might as well keep exploring; she continued along Speedway towards the Marina where the road ended at the Marina channel. To her left a path ran alongside the waterway through a park to the boat slips. To her right, she could push her bike ("No Cycling Allowed") along the jetty, a paved walkway on top of breakwater rocks that separated the channel from the wide sandy beach on the other side. She chose right.

Sailboats headed towards the channel opening and the ocean beyond as she walked along. The tide was out and some children were building a sandcastle on the sandy beach while their mothers gossiped and sunbathed. Stella stopped to watch the children. She closed her eyes, lifted her face to the sun, and felt her shoulders relax. For the first time since arriving in Southern California she really felt she could enjoy a vacation.

The feeling only lasted a minute. A child screamed. Stella's eyes flew open. A little girl was running towards her mother trailing a large piece of seaweed and gesturing towards the rocks. Stella looked down. It was only a few feet to the sand on this side of the breakwater. The tideline was littered with clumps of seaweed. In the one closest to her, wedged up against the rocks, a pale bloated hand reached out from a body covered in slimy greenish-brown tendrils.

CHAPTER 10

"Is it Baywatch? Are they filming?" A middle-aged couple who'd also been strolling along the jetty stopped behind Stella as a lifeguard truck, along with two beach cops on their ATVs, flew across the sand in response to one mother's frantic mobile phone call. She'd started towards the rocks after listening to the child's report, then done a quick turn-around after verifying her daughter's story from a safe distance. The tourist wife pulled out a camera from her beach bag and began snapping away excitedly, babbling about this being an extra bonus to their already fabulous second honeymoon.

Stella set the kickstand, and sat down beside her aunt's bike. Was this real or was it a TV show? She couldn't see any camera crew.

The lifeguard truck and the beach cops followed the group of mothers' and children's pointing fingers towards the jetty. One of the lifeguards got on his two-way radio immediately, and so did one of the beach cops. The other one talked to the moms.

An elderly man walking an overweight chihuahua mix (in spite of the posted "No Dogs" sign) came and stood beside Stella, peering down at the rocks.

"Probably fell off a party boat," he pronounced after glimpsing the body.

The middle-aged honeymooners looked at each other, then at him. "What party boat?"

The elderly man gestured towards the channel on the other side of the breakwater. "They have a boat that goes out at sunset where you can drink and dance the evening away." He nodded towards the seaweed. "Bet he got drunk and fell overboard."

"How d'you know it's a he?" the tourist husband demanded.

Chihuahua Man shrugged.

Stella's eyes strayed back to the mound of seaweed. Now she could see a swollen foot poking out. The toes looked as if they'd been vigorously nibbled, the little one gone entirely. This was a real body, not some dummy in a television segment. *Omigod!*

As the couple and the old man chatted away behind her, a rotting vegetation smell wafted upwards as flies buzzed around the seaweed drying fast in the bright sunlight. From the corner of her eye Stella caught a flash of movement in the rocks. Was that a rat? So much for a beautiful beach scene! She hoped the scenario wouldn't leave the children with lasting nightmares, but they were jumping up and down chattering excitedly to each other as their mothers tried to restrain them from following the police to the breakwater.

Stella's mind flipped back and forth between appalled and fascinated at the same time. *I've never seen a dead body before coming to America. Now it's two, in what, three days? Four? I can't even count any more.* Her eyes were glued to the seaweed in spite of herself. It felt like she was losing track of time as well as her sanity. She started feeling a little dizzy. *Mum would have told me to wear a beach hat* came the unbidden thought.

A patrol car pulled up and parked crosswise to block people from walking out onto the jetty. Two officers walked towards Stella and Chihuahua Man as the couple snapped away. The old man had quickly picked up his dog and tried to zip it into his jacket.

"Don't bother, Howard," one of the approaching officers said. "You know the rules about dogs on the beach."

Apparently, Howard and his pooch were repeat offenders.

"He's on a leash," he replied defensively. "And technically, we're not on the beach."

But the officer's attention was now on the tideline; he raised his hand to the lifeguard and the beach cop inspecting the body before swiveling back to the group on the jetty.

"Hey, didn't I see you somewhere recently?" He looked directly at Stella as his partner continued surveying the rocks and seaweed. "What's your name?" he said sternly.

She instantly felt defensive. "Stella Maris."

"Ah-h yes, the Brit whose aunt fell down the stairs. Whoa."

He caught her shoulder as her knees started to sag before she righted herself.

His partner was instructing Howard and the couple to move back down the breakwater and wait.

"I'm okay," Stella told the officer stoically. *No job, no home, no lover, one too many dead people, and now a questioning by the cops. Again. Can my life get any worse?*

"Yeah, right. Sit down for a minute." The officer turned away from her and spoke into the little radio clipped to his shoulder.

She had a strong impulse to leave, but sat anyway. *This body has nothing to do with me. In no way am I responsible for any of this. It's just a coincidence.* Stella had suddenly forgotten that she didn't believe in coincidences. However, she did recall what the guy who'd sat next to her on the flight to Dallas had said before he departed: "Good luck in the land of fruits and nuts."

Another patrol car arrived and cops started cordoning off the jetty.

"I need to go home." Stella wanted out of the sunshine.

"I need you to tell me some details here first." The officer squatted down beside her, took his notebook out and wrote down her name.

She explained she'd been walking her bike along the jetty, enjoying the sun, then heard a child scream. "I looked down and saw…that." She gestured to the seaweed and started to stand up; her legs felt a little wobbly.

"Are you sure you're all right?" The officer stood and helped steady her as she nodded affirmatively.

"Okay." His look of concern turned into a smile at the corner of his mouth. "I know where to find you if I need any more information." He tapped his notebook. "Try not to find any more dead bodies or I'll start to get suspicious."

Stella was alarmed. *Is that a threat? Or is he flirting with me?* At this point, she couldn't tell the difference. She released the bike stand with a kick as he turned back to the body, and almost mounted to ride off before remembering the "No Cycling" sign for the breakwater. She didn't need a traffic ticket to top this off, but she couldn't wait to get away from the sickening smell wafting up from the rocks. It seemed to be getting worse by the minute in spite of the light breeze.

I need a cup of tea. Stella didn't feel like checking at the Driftwood Street address to see if anyone was there, or cycling back to *Billy's* right away. Instead, she stopped at a little café on Washington Boulevard and sat down in a booth. Nursing a paper cup containing a Lipton's teabag dunked into semi-hot water, she started to feel revived. The tea wasn't good, but it was good enough.

At the next table a young couple were consulting a map. The guy looked up and pointed through the café window. "Entrance to the Venice canals should be about a hundred yards up the street."

He refolded the map as his female companion quickly finished her soda, then they both left. Stella watched them cross the boulevard and walk a short way before making a sharp left by a white fence and disappearing down some steps. She remembered Aunt Barb telling her something about how she and Ron had lived in a little frame house on the canals for a short time during the 1970s. Since then, the remnants of Abbot Kinney's famed waterways had fallen into complete dis-repair, become unnavigable in too many places, and closed to anyone walking through. Recently, though, repairs had been completed and the area was once again open for residents and visitors alike to ramble along the paths.

Stella decided that since the canals were more or less in the direction she'd be heading back to the apartment building, she'd take a scenic walk and see if her aunt's little frame house was still there.

Alas, it was not. A mini-mansion had replaced it. She pushed her bike past a couple of old wooden cottages with roses spilling over their fences. ("No Cycling" along these paths, either.) The canals were charming in spite of new mini-palacios springing up on lots where the original wood-frame houses had been torn down, her aunt's former address being one of the victims to upscale development. Stella recalled what Carol had said about the beach area's gentrification moving down from Santa Monica and up from Redondo Beach, stealthily working its way along the coast from the original working-class neighborhoods.

The Grand Canal had four canals leading off of it at right angles. Stella could have crossed over one of the old wooden bridges to wander further and look around, but since she was thwarted by the "No Cycling" signs, thought it better to come back and explore more another time.

She'd almost reached Venice Boulevard where the waterway had been abruptly blocked off and become a stagnant pool, when she heard raised voices and glanced to her left. Through a gap between two houses she saw Liz standing in the service road running behind the buildings, arms raised in an "I–don't–know" gesture in front of a man who was clearly angry and upset. He banged his fist down on the hood of a Jeep as they argued. The pair hadn't seen Stella, who prudently stifled the greeting she'd almost called out and kept walking. This looked like it might be a lover's tiff.

CHAPTER 11

Stella, along with Gary and some of the residents from *Billy's*, plus a few of Auntie Barb's friends that she'd been able to contact from her address book, were standing on the deck of *Davy Jones Locker* eating sushi and swilling champagne. It wasn't a party boat per se, but it was the funeral party boat for Aunt Barb according to her final wishes.

She'd chosen the music, too. They'd boarded the boat in the Marina to Elvis Presley belting out *My Way*, sailed down the channel to Nat King Cole's *Unforgettable*, and were now heading for the horizon accompanied by Rod Stewart's haunting recording of *Sailing*. Captain Eddie and First Mate Sean had compiled a CD per Aunt Barb's written instructions. Stella had finally made contact with the pair at their business address in the Driftwood Street garage with the help of Mr. Bernstein, Captain Eddie's uncle.

"My older sister's boy," he'd explained on the phone. "Your aunt was fond of him."

Now, Mr. Bernstein stood on the boat popping a piece of California roll into his mouth. He'd provided a case of Veuve Clicquot per his client and friend's last instructions, even though the will had merely stipulated champagne.

"She deserved some of the better stuff," he'd maintained.

When Stella had invited him to the funeral, he'd replied: "I wouldn't miss it for the world."

Her mother had been a different story. Jim's back surgery had been successful, but he and Sheila were stuck at their holiday condo in Spain for a few weeks more.

"I'm exhausted," her mother had said when Stella had rung to let her know about Barbara's funeral. "I've been fetching and carrying ever since Jim was discharged from the hospital." She mimicked her husband's whining. "I need a softer pillow; close the curtains, it's too light in here. Open the curtains; it's too dark in here. I want lemonade instead of water. I need another pain pill." Sheila sighed. "What am I? Florence Nightingale all of a sudden? I've checked the insurance policy to see if they'll pay for nurse visits or some sort of home help, but it doesn't look like it. I can't do all this by myself! I'm supposed to be on vacation!"

Me, too. Stella sympathized with her mother. Jim, too, after all it was his vacation as well. While talking to Sheila, she'd had a vision of herself at nine years old, ill in bed. Her mother comforting her as always, but for twenty-four hours, tops. After that, Sheila's bedside manner would go into decline, rapidly defaulting to assuring Stella that she was better and it was time to get up. *She's always been like this; she'll never change.*

"I'm sorry, darling, but I can't possibly make it over there." Sheila sounded rueful, yet conflicted. "You know I'd like to help you out, but you seem to have things under control."

They talked a little more, but before Stella could tell her mother further details contained in Auntie Barb's will, the part about leaving everything to her "dear niece Stella" she heard Jim's voice calling out in the background.

"Sheila, I need you!"

"Gotta go, sweetie." And her mother hung up.

Stella's attention switched back to the funeral party boat when she heard Gary Edwards opining that the body from the breakwater had gone into the ocean north of the Marina and drifted south with the current before getting washed up by the rocks.

"An officer in the Pacific Division substation told my life-guard friend that the coroner estimated it could have been in the water for a few days up to a week."

"Perhaps it floated down from Malibu," Carol suggested.

"Nah." Gary was doubtful. "Estimating ocean temperature and drift, along with the medical examiner's report, the cops and lifeguards came up with south of the Santa Monica pier."

Carol shrugged. "Maybe Venice then."

"Or Ocean Park," Greg offered.

"From the state of the guy's body, verdict was he'd drowned and been swept out to sea," Gary continued. "Any marks on him were due to ocean creatures dining out. They'd chewed off part of his face, too."

"Ughh," Liz shuddered.

She was attending the funeral solo, Stella noted.

"Do they know who the dead body was?" Carol declined a fresh plate of sushi being passed around.

"Not yet," Gary answered, also shaking his head at the raw fish delicacy.

First Mate Sean emerged from the galley with a plate of hot sausage rolls.

"This is so like Barbara," Carol commented, accepting one and biting into it.

"She planned everything down to the last detail," Stella said, sipping her champagne. *Aunt Barb didn't know her plans would be implemented sooner rather than later.* She shook her head at the sausage rolls as well as the sushi; she didn't feel like eating.

As they sailed into twilight, the conversation drifted between saying nice things about Stella's late aunt: "She was always understanding if you were a bit late with the rent" (Liz), back to speculation about the body found by the rocks: "It could have been a tourist caught in a riptide."

This was uttered by Andrea, the woman sans underwear who'd jumped on her lover's bicycle after their bird call duet. Andrea was on the boat with her next-door apartment neighbor, Sam. Carol had told Stella they didn't actually live together, but he'd cut a doorway between their apartments downstairs via the adjoining wall closet soon after Andrea had moved in. It was becoming clear to Stella that this was a bunch of wayward tenants; Aunt Barb had certainly believed in "live and let live." She wondered if Sam knew about the bird-calling guy on the bike. Or vice versa.

"Okay, folks. Time for the main event." Captain Eddie cut the motor.

Mr. Bernstein made sure everyone's champagne glass was refilled. First Mate Sean stepped to the prow of the boat and lit a taper. He and Captain Eddie had deftly mixed Auntie Barb's cremated remains with black powder and oxidizing agents along with other added chemicals. Aunt Barb had chosen their business for the final part of her funeral arrangements because she liked the name: "Go Out With A Bang."

The very last part of Stella's aunt shot skywards to the strains of Led Zeppelin's *Stairway to Heaven.* Shrieking rockets burst into showers of exploding flower fountains and shooting stars to the "oohs," "ahhs," whistles and cheers of those on board. Gary Edwards saluted as the music morphed into Judy Garland singing *Somewhere, Over the Rainbow*.

Then everybody hushed as a blue whale slid by close to the boat.

"Whale migrating season," Carol murmured.

"Largest mammal on earth," Gary added quietly.

Everyone else was silent.

If it decides to surface we're doomed, Stella couldn't help thinking, both afraid and in awe at the sight of this wild creature.

After the giant had passed, she lifted her champagne glass as remnants of shooting stars fell like teardrops into the waves. *We're all just specks in the universe.*

As the last of the champagne was poured, the sun compressed itself into a coral disc and shot a phosphorus glow into the evening sky. The waters rolled into the curvature of the earth and night descended.

"Bon voyage, Aunt Barbara," Stella said.

Everyone lifted their glasses.

"Bon voyage, Aunt Barbara," they echoed, adding a few last-minute testimonials before starting to sing along to Bob Dylan's *Knockin' On Heaven's Door*. Captain Eddie restarted the engine and turned the boat back to port.

They were still singing—the music had changed to Leonard Cohen's *Hallelujah*—although they were now drunkenly swaying in unison. *Davy Jones Locker* re-entered the Marina channel and docked. Aunt Barbara's funeral party participants stumbled down the gangplank to Vera Lynn's famous World War II song, *We'll Meet Again*.

But it wasn't over yet.

Back at *Billy's* the strings of patio lights had all been turned on. Tina Turner belted out *Simply The Best* from loudspeakers hooked up from one of the apartments via an open bathroom window as votive candles were lit and floated in the goldfish pond. Liz brought out a punchbowl of her homemade sangria with apple and orange slices floating on the top and placed it on the patio table; chairs were moved aside and a space was cleared for dancing. Gary had provided a plate of his mother's tea sandwiches. Andrea contributed an arugula salad, and Carol added a platter of deviled eggs.

Stella phoned in for pizza delivery as a swelling number of guests arrived. Aunt Barb had not specified a bash at *Billy's* in her funeral wishes, but heck, this was the post-funeral party party, Stella reasoned. And why not? It seemed the whole neighborhood was turning up. She just hoped Vi and Edna wouldn't deign to attend.

It was a noisy crowd. Liz had put on music with a salsa beat and pretty soon the throng of friends and neighbors were gyrating to something between a Latin conga and a line dance. The tenant who lived in the apartment next to Liz, who had introduced herself to Stella as Cindy, joined in holding her small dog esconced in a baby sling across her chest, making the little animal's head jiggle along to the music. Stella, who was now feeling quite happy and very drunk on her third glass of sangria since Liz kept topping it up, saw Mr. Velvet sitting up on the porch railing; she swore he had a disapproving look in his eye. *Maybe it's not the people or the party; maybe he just doesn't like that dog.* She reflected on Howard at the Marina jetty zipping his chihuahua into his jacket and thought about small dogs being referred to as lap dogs in days gone by. Or was it just that people of a certain age in Los Angeles carried them around like babies?

"Are all the tenants here?" Stella asked Carol who seemed to know almost everyone, but then she had mentioned in their first meeting that she'd lived at *Billy's* a long time.

"Everyone except the guy who lives above Liz, next door to Greg. He's either working or staying over with his girlfriend."

Stella noticed Andrea was sitting very close to Sam. "Are those two really an item?"

Carol shrugged. "She has a husband, you know."

"What!"

"And two kids. They live somewhere else."

Maybe he was the guy on the bike–maybe Andrea was two-timing her boyfriend with her husband.

"Does the husband ride a bike?" She couldn't help asking.

"Oh, no. That's someone else," Carol replied. "That's her artist-lover."

How do people do that? Have several lovers at one time and keep their names straight? What if you slipped up in a moment of passion–or inebriation?

"Isn't he an artist?" Stella nodded toward Sam who had picked up a guitar and was softly strumming it.

"Only technically," Carol conceded. "He's her musician-lover. The one with the bike, he's her artist–lover, he paints."

Stella digested this bit of information. "How many lovers does she have?"

Carol shrugged again. "Who knows."

Stella looked around the funeral partygoers/wake attendees noticing Gary couldn't take his eyes off Liz. *He's in love with her.* But Liz wasn't looking back at Gary. She was looking daggers at Andrea, who was looking adoringly at Sam. Stella sighed. Who could explain the human heart? *More likely it's the human brain. The whole world runs on hormones.*

Greg helped himself to a glass of sangria and looked around the patio after he took a sip. More chairs were being brought out from people's apartments; some were sitting on the raised ledge of the goldfish pond while others leaned against the wall of the grocery building next door.

"If people from another time or another planet landed here, I wonder what they'd think?" he mused out loud.

"They'd probably take off and go back to where they'd come from right away," Carol replied.

"My cat's missing." Greg changed the subject.

"Hitler? Haven't seen him." Carol was drinking bottled water.

Stella felt a giggle coming on. *I've drunk too much. Feels good, though.* Liz had joined the line-dance and held out a hand to her. She put her empty glass down and went to join the salsa beat under the starlit sky. It was the last thing she remembered.

Sometime early in the morning, she woke up on the bathroom floor. She vaguely remembered spending most of the night there clutching the toilet bowl. *Too much alcohol, not enough to eat?* Her stomach ached, she had a bad headache, and someone was knocking on the back door. It was Carol.

"Everyone's got food poisoning."

CHAPTER 12

Well, not everyone. Carol reported she was fine. And so was Gary Edwards.

"It must've been the sushi."

Stella detected an accusatory tone in Carol's voice. *Maybe it was your deviled eggs.* She couldn't remember eating anything much the night before. "It could've been a topping on one of the pizzas," she said instead. "Excuse me."

Stella rushed for the bathroom and threw up. Carol had prudently removed herself by the time Stella finally re-emerged. Mr. Velvet was sitting expectantly by his empty dish on the kitchen floor. He blinked at her.

"I don't care what time it is or even what day it is, I'm going to bed," she told him, taking a box of Kitty Kibbles from the pantry shelf. It had an image on the front of a cat wearing a ten-gallon hat and cowboy boots reaching for a gun from a holster slung around its furry hips. "You're in charge."

After she filled the cat dish, her stomach still ached, though not as badly as it had. *I think I'm still a little drunk. Or something.* Stella staggered into the other room, pulled down the bed and collapsed into a deep sleep.

The phone ringing woke her up. Mr. Bernstein was calling to tell her what a great time he'd had at Aunt Barbara's funeral. "She would've loved it," he told Stella. "You did a great job." His tone changed to one of concern. "Are you okay? You sound like you've got a bad hangover."

"I've got a headache and I've been throwing up." She told him about the food poisoning. "Carol's blaming the sushi."

"I ate it, and I'm fine," he retorted,

Stella mentioned she hadn't eaten any, and she wasn't fine.

"Then it couldn't have been the sushi," he said. "You're off the hook for liability. It must've been something else."

Since Stella hadn't eaten a sausage roll, and Mr. Bernstein as well as Carol had, they agreed that couldn't have been the culprit, either. Bad champagne was dismissed as a non-starter as well as all other alcohol. Together they ran down the list of food served at *Billy's*.

"Everyone contributed," Mr. Bernstein pointed out. "It's not your fault."

High on the suspect list according to Mr. Bernstein were the tea sandwiches contributed by Gary's mother. "Some of them had ham chopped into mayonnaise. I didn't touch those."

"Me, either," Stella agreed, recalling she actually hadn't eaten much since breakfast except for a teensy-weensy piece of cheese pizza and a couple of bites of arugula salad. Maybe it was the red pepper flakes someone had sprinkled on top of the pizza. She wasn't used to that and hadn't cared much for it at all. Who'd done that? She couldn't recall, and now it bothered her.

"But you drank the sangria which had some apple slices floating on the top."

Stella admitted she'd been very liberal on that score, but she didn't remember eating any fruit.

"If any of Barbara's friends and other neighbors became ill, I'm sure you'll hear about it," the lawyer remarked. "You can ask them what they ate and drank."

Or if anyone died!

But the lawyer was now bringing legal matters up to date. "I'll be filing the will with the Probate Court soon. Keep checking your aunt's mailbox for any incoming bills."

Stella shook off her suspicious mind and told him about Greg and the deal he had with her aunt about taking the stairs rebuilding costs off of his rent.

"Fine. Just send me the Post-it and anything else written down when you're feeling better. And by the way, don't be so formal. Call me Harry."

"Okay. Harry." Stella felt her intestines cramping again. "I've got to go," she told him.

"Take care of yourself. I'll call you tomorrow to see how you're doing," he replied and they both hung up.

When Stella emerged from the bathroom she made herself a cup of weak tea and a slice of toast, no butter. It was her mother's nausea remedy.

Sheila rang just as Stella finished her decidedly unexciting meal and was thinking about going back to bed.

"You sound hungover," her mother said suspiciously.

"No, just tired," Stella lied. One didn't admit flagrant drunkenness to one's mother so she quickly brought Sheila up to date on how well the funeral had gone, then changed the subject. "How's Jim? Got any help yet?"

Stella was fond of her mother's second husband, but it was a good digression because (a) she wasn't in the mood to discuss anything about Barbara's will or business affairs to Sheila right this minute, (b) was genuinely uncertain how things would work out since she felt she hadn't had enough time to make up her mind about her life yet, and (c) one didn't tell one's mother everything. Plus, Sheila had seemed a little too overjoyed that Stella and Brian had broken up since she'd always considered him a waste of space, that Stella could do much better in the boyfriend department.

"Yes, but it's not enough. The woman just comes for an hour in the mornings, and I need someone in the afternoons, too."

She heard Jim calling for her mother in the background. "I better let you go."

"All right. Just give me a call when you're coming back. You can always stay with us for a few days."

Maybe. At that moment, Stella couldn't think that far ahead.

The tea and toast revived her. The stomach ache was gone. She hadn't mentioned the food poisoning to Sheila, either.

Stella had been so busy seeing to her aunt's affairs, she'd almost forgotten about Olivia's invitation to her art opening which was due to start in a couple of hours. Fishing for the artist's business card in her handbag she dialed her home number.

"I'm not going to make it." Stella explained the circumstances.

"No problem." Olivia was very sympathetic. "Why don't you come by my house when you're feeling better? I'm usually at home because my studio's there, too."

"I'd like that."

They chatted a bit more and Olivia gave her the address. "Call me when you're coming and I'll show you my paintings.

Right now, I have to go. I have to get some wine on the way to the gallery. It puts people in a better frame of mind when they're looking at art with a glass of chardonnay in their hands."

Carol was knocking on the kitchen door again. Stella waved her in as she hung up.

"I've come to see if you need anything. Are you feeling any better?"

"Just a little hollow inside, but the pain's subsided." Stella indicated the overstuffed armchair. "Have a seat. Oh."

It was already occupied by Mr. Velvet, who'd curled up and was fast asleep on the lumpy cushions after his breakfast and hadn't moved a muscle since. Aunt Barb's apartment was painted white, including the bookshelf running around the walls in the dining-room and living room/bedroom. It looked very clean, but also very funky. Yet somehow the armchair's flower-patterned upholstery didn't clash with the zebra-patterned rug covering the painted floorboards.

"This'll do." Carol pulled out a chair and sat down at the dining table opposite Stella. "I wanted to talk to you about something else, also."

Stella hoped it was something other than food poisoning or the rent. Although she was feeling better, she was not in the mood for any type of discussion.

"Would you mind if there was another little celebration of life for your aunt? Some of Barbara's friends couldn't make it last night, but they'd like to note her passing. They–we," Carol amended," want to have a special little ceremony to honor her memory."

Stella was touched. No wonder her aunt had stayed in California. Her friends and acquaintances obviously thought more of her than her immediate family. Still, how many parties could you have for a dead person?

"You mean like a post-funeral party party?"

"Yeah, by her women's group."

"Women's group?" This was new.

"Our special women's group that Barbara belonged to," Carol explained. "Hecate's Hags."

"Hecate's Hags?" Stella could imagine Aunt Barb as a hippie once upon a time, but she couldn't imagine her as a hag.

"Witches," Carol extrapolated.

Stella knew she was in a weakened state, but it was at this moment that she felt she'd really stepped through the looking glass into an adventure she hadn't asked for. True, she'd taken up her aunt's invitation to come and visit "sometime" in an impetuous moment of distress, but said invite had implied a vacation, a gift. A birthday gift. A gift that had turned into a series of nightmarish and crazy events. There'd been a fork in the road of her life and she was on it, with or without her consent. *What the heck?*

"Okay," she nodded to Carol. "I'm sure Aunt Barb would approve."

"You're invited, of course," Carol beamed.

"When is it?"

"Tomorrow."

CHAPTER 13

Dockweiler Beach was directly under the flight path of LAX at the end of the runway. Planes were taking off from the airport at a rapid pace, climbing into the evening sky and heading out over the ocean before turning in the direction of their intended destinations. Every time a plane flew over the noise was so tremendous it obliterated all other sounds for a few minutes. Waves pounding onto the beach took care of the in-between moments ensuring a complete and rare kind of privacy right out in the open.

"It's the only place you can have a fire on a Los Angeles County beach," Carol had explained. "Otherwise, we'd have to drive up past Malibu and over the line into Ventura County which is too far. Dockweiler's the closest to us."

"Do I have to wear anything special?" Stella thought she'd have to rifle through Aunt Barb's closet if cloaks and masks were required.

"No. Just wear something warm," Carol had advised. "It can get cold on the beach at night. Jeans and a sweater will do."

Not Druid-y type witches, then. Although Stella had never met her aunt since the woman had never gone back to England for a visit after she left all those years ago, she still couldn't imagine her as a witch.

"We're a coven," Carol had explained. "Goddesses in the ancient world."

Looks more like a support group. Stella watched as half-a-dozen middle-aged women unpacked their rattles and prayer sticks. Someone had even brought a packet of graham crackers along with a bag of marshmallows and an extra-value sized bar of chocolate "for our snack," she explained.

Carol was busy throwing wood into the fire pit and lighting it. The stack looked suspiciously like planks from the old steps at *Billy's*, the staircase Aunt Barb had met her untimely demise on.

She confirmed it. "We're burning them to clear out any nasty vibes. Fire's a purification."

So–a true cleansing. This whole goddess ritual thing was beginning to make sense to Stella. After all, she reasoned, several cultures around the world believed in fire as purification. She threw a handful of sage leaves Carol had provided onto the wood as the flames caught. A musty, earthy smell arose from the smoke, almost medicinal. The women wafted it towards themselves with both hands, guiding it over their head and shoulders, breathing in deeply.

Carol had explained the name of their group to Stella on the drive over to Dockweiler. "Hecate was a Greek goddess of earth, sea and sky.

A broad spectrum goddess, then.

"Also, the Goddess of Crossroads, plus she was worshipped as one of the protectors of the household in ancient Athens," Carol continued, turning into the beach parking lot.

Crossroads sounded right on target. *Maybe I'm in the right place after all–deciding to visit Los Angeles. Just because I've never experienced anything like this doesn't mean to say it's strange.*

"Just stand next to me and follow along." Carol extracted a turtle shell from her backpack with strings of colored beads dangling from where the live animal's legs had once been. She placed it on the sand by her feet, then pulled out a short piece of bamboo wrapped with decorative stripes of colored wool that ended in a cluster of brown seed pods. They rattled as Carol laid it down by Stella's feet.

"Yours for the ceremony. Okay, wimmin. Ready?"

Everyone raised their arms to the night sky. Stella reached up, too.

"We start by invoking the four directions to create the magic circle," Carol muttered. "It creates a safe space where we can experience our inner selves more deeply."

Stella wasn't sure she was ready to experience her inner self more deeply; it was in danger of being overwhelmed lately. Too much chaos around her. Still, this was fun, and it made her feel a little closer to Aunt Barb.

"Goddesses of the East!" Carol called out, leading off the opening incantation in a moment of quiet before the next plane took off.

The women turned to the east.

"Elements of air..." Carol continued.

"...mind and breath," one of the other women added.

"Dawning light!" Someone shouted.

"Awakening of ideas!"

"Be with us," Carol concluded.

A jumbo jet flew overhead, its wheels tucking back into its belly as it ascended into the night sky. Stella wished she'd worn ear plugs. She wondered why they weren't doing this in "the dawning light." *It would be easier during daytime, but, then they wouldn't have the fire, an important component of their plan. Or the snack part with the 'Smores.*

Carol waited until echoes of the take-off had vanished into the night sky, then the group turned another ninety degrees.

"Goddesses of the South! Fire Goddess! Pele! Passion! Ang-gerrrr!"

Another plane was coming.

"E-N-E-R-G-Y!" Two people shouted in unison.

There was a moment of quiet after the plane passed, then everyone turned another ninety degrees to face the waves on the shoreline.

"Goddesses of the West! Water Goddesses! O-S-H-U-N! Eee-mo-SHUN! Be with us," Carol shouted above the din of an Alaska Airlines flight.

The women turned a final ninety degrees.

"Goddesses of the North! Earth Goddesses!"

"Growth! Decay! New Growth!"

"Birth and Death!"

"Renewal and endings!"

"Mystery—the unseen!"

Silence. Nobody had anything else to add.

"The circle is now closed!"

The goddesses lowered their arms and Carol handed a bottle of Evian around "for libation." Each goddess took a sip and/or sprinkled a few drops on the flames in the fire pit making them sizzle.

A woman picked up her gourd drum and started a beat. Others picked up their rattles keeping time as they sung. Stella followed along, shaking the bamboo stick, making the seed pods sound like rain falling on a tin roof. The chanting began.

"Isis Astarte Diana Hecate Demeter Kali...Inana."

Then the beat changed.

"We all come from the Goddess/And to her we shall return/Like a drop of rain/Falling to the o-o-ocean."

They chanted and sang, celebrating Aunt Barbara's life as the moon rose high above them and people flew through the air to destinations around the globe. Personal remembrances of her were shared and someone recited a short poem to her life. Tears were shed. Stella was touched. Her aunt had been loved and admired by friends and acquaintances more than her own family. And people had been so nice to Stella since she'd arrived. She relaxed. Really, there was nothing she couldn't cope with, whatever happened.

Marshmallows were toasted on straightened wire coat hangers, then slapped onto graham crackers with a piece of chocolate. One woman objected to the snack as "over the top," but she was voted down. The women sat on the sand and shared a personal problem or two about families and work as they ate and chatted. Stella inquired if any of them had been at Aunt Barb's funeral. No-one had. She then asked Carol who, exactly, had mentioned an upset stomach.

"Liz reported mild abdominal discomfort to me," Carol remembered, "but then she eats untouched leftovers from people's plates at the restaurant." Cindy had mentioned a stomach ache, and Sam, Andrea and Greg reported not feeling too well.

"I suppose they could have drunk too much," Carol added as an afterthought.

Maybe. Stella wasn't entirely sure.

After a couple of hours, the women stood around the fire pit again, held hands, and Carol declared the circle "open but unbroken." Arms were lifted in unison to a mighty shout, the fire was doused with the rest of the Evian, and Hecate's Hags started packing up to go home,

Stella wandered down to the water's edge, slipped off her sandals, and dipped her feet into the edge of the waves. Lights from other fire pits and jets taking off above her cast small illuminated pools that rippled over the dark sea. She didn't believe in coincidences, but her experience of food poisoning joined the list of recent coincidences: her aunt's slip-and-fall, that vehicle in the parking lot almost running Stella down, and the suspicion someone had been in the apartment when she arrived home. Not to mention Gary Edwards spying on her from his darkened house next door the night she arrived. But perhaps the police and paramedic activity had awakened him, she reasoned. True, he'd looked a little weird in his surgeon's coat and beach hat, not to mention the goggles and chainsaw when she'd met him fixing a new surfboard in daylight, but he'd seemed normal enough at the funeral. *Am I in danger from someone? But why?*

A small shell washed over her toes. She picked it up for a closer look. An ornate scallop, *Pecten ornatus,* creamy white with a pinkish circumference around its heart-shaped edge that was usually found in warmer waters Carol told her as they trudged back across the beach. *This shell must have been blown north by strong currents, driven by the waves.* Stella put it in her pocket.

Shhahh shhahh. Shhahh shhahh. The breath of the night wind, the breath of the night sea. The breath of the earth in darkness as Stella lay dreaming. The sea washed over the shore and waves from the other side of the world rolled onto Venice Beach in a strong briny smell that permeated drifting swathes of fog. Shhahh shhahh. The spirit of the Night Mother breathed over Venice rooftops, rustling palm trees on the Boardwalk.

Shzzahh shzzahh. A rollerblader gliding home on Speedway from his late-night job at the Boardwalk Café stirred Stella's sleeping form as she wandered in Dreamtime, that landscape of the third realm which tells us truths we hide from ourselves in daylight.

Shhahh shhahh, the twinkling of stars and planets, the rattle of seashells as The Night Mother emerged from the dark sky, constellations shining through her robes. Gauzy layers floated out from her dark yet luminous body in swathes of blue on black, shot through with glimpses of sunset and colors of twilight, the sand shining mylar pink footprints from feet that never touched the ground. She had seaweed and pieces of coral, periwinkles and ammonites, lightning welks and calico scallops woven through her long tresses with coquina clams and jingle shells making haunting music as she advanced. She shimmered. She sparkled. She spoke. The Night Mother was enormous and very beautiful, but she also sounded very, very strict.

"Read the book. Read the book," she breathed huskily, pointing a long finger at Stella, her voice as deep as the ocean undulating in satiny waves over the earth. "Read the book, the little black book."

What little black book?

Stella was transfixed. The Night Mother looked like Auntie Barb for a split second, then her features changed and Aunt Barb's face disappeared as The Night Mother started receding into the Milky Way.

"Read the book, Stella! Read the book. And wake up!" she called over her shoulder, leaving behind the sound of tinkling seashells on the night breeze as she vanished.

What book? Come back!

Zzahh zzahh. Headlights on Speedway, car tires on asphalt slowing down outside *Billy's.*

Thwack! The morning newspaper hit the apartment steps. Stella woke up, her eyes blinking at the book shelf traversing the bedroom walls. And then she saw it. A little black book. She sat up as she spied another one. And another. There were a dozen or more little black books without any writing on the spine scattered amongst the novels and paperbacks on the shelf that ran around the room, interrupted only by the Murphy bed, the window and the door into the closet. And as she looked through the doorway into the other room, she saw more black books on the shelf running around the walls in there.

Bloody hell! Which little black book!?!

CHAPTER 14

Stella stared at the walls as she sat at the dining-room table eating her bowl of breakfast Cheerios. Apart from breaks for the dining-room window, the other Murphy bed in the apartment, the kitchen doorway, bathroom and front doors, plus the built-in credenza with glass-fronted cupboards on top, little black books were tucked in between How-To titles and authors who claimed to have the spiritual answer to life's problems on the shelf that ran around all four walls. Stella's eyes lit on one: *Truth or Dare* by someone named Starhawk. She smiled to herself. How very Auntie Barb. But which little black book could the Night Mother have been referring to? If, indeed, that dream had meant anything at all.

Stella sighed and looked out of the window which she'd continued to leave open because it was warm enough to do that in Southern California (compared to February's icy blasts in England), plus, she liked the faint sound of the ocean wafting through the apartment, especially at night, and after all, it was Mr. Velvet's cat door.

At there he was, sitting in the pine tree looking back at her with his green eyes. She smiled; he was very cute, very pretty for a boy cat. What would happen to him when she went back to England? He sprung from the branch onto the dining-room table, purring as he started rubbing his face against her arm.

She kissed the top of his head. "I suppose you want breakfast."

He gave his standard reply: "Miaow."

Stella finished her Cheerios and pushed the bowl towards him to lap up the milk residue, before going into the kitchen and putting the kettle on to boil for tea. While the water heated, she walked back into the dining-room, plucked one of the little back books off the shelf at random and opened it.

"Barbara Smith's Diary, Summer 1976" her aunt had inscribed inside. Stella turned the page and started reading. It had been written while Aunt Barb was traveling across Canada seventeen years before making observations such as: *'The water around Montreal is so polluted you can't bathe in it. In August, it stinks. People are afraid to go sailing for fear their boat will cap-size, they'll end up in the water and it'll kill them."*

She then went on to write that one in two Canadians were overweight, adding *"I can't say that they're any worse than the Americans,"* although she thought Americans were taller. *"Canadian men are short. Especially French-Canadian men."'*

Stella frowned. Auntie Barb was sounding too much like Sheila here. Judgmental. She wondered if her mother had known Ray, her sister's long-time partner, then husband, was Canadian. Stella didn't remember anyone ever mentioning it.

Flipping through a few more pages, she read about her aunt's visit to a nightclub: *"I danced with a Mountie, a real Dudley Do-Right! He said he's plain-clothes division, but I like to think there's a little red uniform jacket and a pair of jodhpurs hiding in his wardrobe. Currently guarding the Queen of England during her visit, his job mainly consists of looking for the one person or persons in the crowd who are looking the other way, not at her, not in the direction everyone else is looking. Usually, he works in drugs. Then he said he shouldn't be telling me this."*

Too late. Auntie Barb had dutifully recorded it in her diary, along with his name and the fact she'd given him her phone number. Stella's aunt might be gone now, but her life was left behind for anyone to see. Her impressions of Canada had been followed by that week's grocery list and an itemization of expenditures incurred in her travels. Stella closed the diary and put it back on the shelf. She had a feeling that it wasn't the one the Night Mother had recommended.

She made a pot of tea and selected another little black book before sitting down at the table. Inside, it was dated the summer of 1969; Barbara was in New York where the temperature was too high, the air too humid, and she felt like a piece of sweating cheese under a glass-domed cheese dish. This didn't seem like the right "little black book," either.

Stella wondered if the diaries were in any particular order. She stood up and grabbed another one farther along on the shelf. It was undated and started out complaining about her relationship with Ray that went on for several pages. This unhappiness sounded a bit too familiar to Stella in her current state. Ray had been dead for several years so this diary must have been written prior to 1990, three years before. She stuck it back on the shelf.

Stella wondered about the dream. On one hand she wanted to determine what it meant because dreams were considered important on many levels in so many societies since time began. But, which little black book could the Night Mother be referring to? She had said "book" singular, not "books" plural.

Stella's eyes flitted round the bookshelves as she drank her tea and mentally noted the number of plain black covers. Too many. *I have a lot of reading ahead of me.*

She felt a shred of despair creeping in. True, the diaries were a chance to find out who her aunt had been and how she had lived her life–something the family knew very little of, or didn't much care about–but Stella started to feel overwhelmed and daunted because it wasn't just one little black book. There were just so many of them it seemed like a chore, like she was back at school and this was an extended biography reading project with a horrid test involved somewhere along the way. What's more, the books weren't exactly little. The Canadian journal contained 214 closely handwritten pages. And no double spacing. Barbara Smith had favored artist sketchbooks to write in, approximately 5x8 with unlined pages that fortunately she'd numbered by hand. *And what exactly am I looking for apart from a fuller version of Aunt Barb's life? And why?*

Stella sensed that there was some kind of pressure regarding time and it was important that she get it right. She had to choose the right book. That's if she accepted the dream's challenge. Stella felt she should; she owed it to her aunt on some level. After all, she'd been gifted with an apartment building and was using Barbara's money to fund her vacation expenses.

Stella finished her tea, walked into the bedroom, and after putting the Murphy bed away started checking the dates on the diaries on the shelf in there. One contained two books written in the early 1980s, then 1968, 1974, and 1989. They were shelved in no particular order, as if Barbara had deliberately scattered them among her regular books so they would be hidden in plain sight. Why would she do that? Aunt Barb didn't seem like a sloppy person; her files were orderly in the filing cabinet. Clothes were neatly hung in the closet. Towels were folded and everything was tidied away in the bathroom cabinet. *She's better organized than I am.* Stella thought back to her aunt's will and funeral. *All the way round.* So contrary to what her mother had always inferred about her "hippie younger sister." Had she done it on purpose? Who was she hiding something from, and why?

Stella shook her head and went to open the window shades. It was a beautiful day outside. *Time for a different approach.* She stood in the middle of the room, arms outstretched and closed her eyes, then spun in a circle before opening them again after she stopped. Her left arm pointed towards one wall which she quickly scanned. No little black books on that shelf. She looked in the other direction where her arm pointed right. Aha! Past the end of her fingertips she spied a little black book amongst all the paperbacks. She plucked it off the shelf, ignoring two others further along. She had to start somewhere and this one would do. Inside her aunt had written: *January 1991 – I'm about to become a property owner!*

Stella quickly scanned the page depicting some details of the deal Aunt Barb and Bill Craven were discussing about Barbara purchasing *Billy's* apartment building.

Why am I standing here in the middle of the room reading this? Stella quickly changed into her bikini and sandals, grabbed one of her aunt's loose summer dresses from the closet, as well as her floppy straw hat and a striped beach bag, tossed the diary inside the bag along with a beach towel and a bottle of sunscreen from the bathroom cabinet, then picked up her sunglasses from the credenza before heading out through the kitchen door stopping only for a bottle of water from the refrigerator and to fill Mr. Velvet's bowl with *Kitty*

Kibbles. After firmly locking the back door she went down the now-sturdy new steps Greg had built, through the garden and crossed the Boardwalk onto the white sandy beach, where she settled down on the towel to work on her California tan as she read her aunt's diary.

It wasn't very interesting at first, full of language about appraisals and loans before Barbara and Bill had decided to forego convention and keep it simple. She would give Bill a cash lump sum from her husband Ray's life insurance keeping a portion for herself, some of her and Ray's savings, then send Bill half of the monthly payments from the rents until the agreed-upon price was paid off. Barbara had estimated she wouldn't need much for monthly expenses as there were royalty checks from the musician's union coming in regularly as well as small dividends from investments. Aunt Barb had sketched out the terms in her diary in purple ink. Stella hoped there was a finalized and notarized signed agreement in the filing cabinet. She hadn't thought to ask Harry Bernstein if he had a copy of that document. *It must have been above board; it's now 1993, so that was two years ago when the deal was made.*

Stella yawned. The sun was nice and warm; the breeze off of the ocean softly caressing her skin. She'd look in the filing cabinet later. Stella lay back on the towel and closed her eyes.

CHAPTER 15

She woke up to the sound of nearby beach umbrellas flapping loudly in the wind; the breeze had picked up and the waves had whitecaps. Stella poked her arm with a fingertip. It was a little pink. *Time to go back to the apartment.*

As Stella opened the gate in the white picket fence, she realized she needed to check her aunt's mailbox per the lawyer's request. There might be something in there that needed attention. She pulled out the bunch of her aunt's keys from the straw bag and stopped in at the front building where the mailboxes were located. Number 8 was loaded with junk mail envelopes and flyers, plus a few bills, which she'd pass on to Harry Bernstein. *Have to look for the building's sale documents and talk to him about those, too.*

As she came out and turned to walk through the garden, someone called to her.

"Stella? Stella Maris?"

She looked up. A man about her own age or a little older was standing on the Boardwalk by the front gate, a backpack over one shoulder. He looked familiar, but she couldn't immediately place him.

"Yes."

"Stella, it's Nigel."

His name didn't ring a bell.

"Brian's, er, friend–with the pub."

She continued staring at him blankly. *He's very good-looking.* Then it dawned. *The boyfriend stealer!*

"What the hell are you doing here?

Nigel blinked nervously. "It's a bit of a story."

Of course it is. "Is Brian with you?" She looked around as if he might be in tow, then belatedly realized she might not recognize her former boyfriend if he was in his Doris the barmaid incarnation.

"No, he's back in England, minding the pub."

"So, what are you doing here again?"

"I could ask you the same thing."

Stella felt herself bristling. *Bloody cheek. Who did he think he was? Is my ex-lover and his new boyfriend checking up on me?* She was steaming inside. *Did Brian call my mother to find out where I was and then send his paramour to talk to me? Surely not. Better not have!*

Nigel glanced up at *Billy's.* "Are you visiting someone?"

"That was the intent."

Nigel nodded understandingly. "Vacation?"

None of your bloody business! Wait, was he about to offer some sort of apology for stealing the man she'd been living with for five years?

"What do you want?"

"This is just, um, amazing to bump into you like this. I mean, what a coincidence. This is crazy!"

Nigel ran his fingers through his hair, which was untidy to begin with, then rubbed his eyes with both hands. Stella felt herself calming down; he seemed rather distraught.

"I haven't slept in a couple of days. I arrived in Los Angeles at the crack of dawn and had an absolutely horrendous encounter with the police. I feel as if I'm about to pass out."

Yes, the LA cops can be something else.

"My brother died." Nigel blinked back tears.

"Oh, I'm sorry." Stella didn't know what to say. Was she really sorry? He did look green around the gills. She defaulted to the standard English safety net which covered all occasions.

"Would you like a cup of tea?"

"That would be lovely."

He sounded so grateful and relieved that Stella forgot he was her enemy and started to really feel sorry for him. She opened the gate and led him down the garden path and up the stairs to Aunt Barb's.

Nigel slumped down at the dining-room table and looked around as Stella put the kettle on to boil.

"This little flat is terrific!"

"It belongs to my aunt."

"Lucky lady."

"She died."

"Oh, I'm sorry." Now it was Nigel's turn to not know what to say.

They were both quiet as Stella made a fresh pot of tea and brought it to the table. She'd even opened a packet of shortbreads.

"Biscuits!" Nigel eyed the plate hungrily.

"Help yourself." She pushed the plate towards him.

Nigel took four, which constituted half the plate, and bit one in half as he glanced out the window.

"There's a cat in that tree!"

He swallowed a mouthful of shortbread while staring incredulously at Mr. Velvet, who sprang from a branch and onto the table. Purring loudly, he presented himself to Nigel for petting.

"I love cats!"

Mr. Velvet rubbed up against Nigel as he stroked his head.

Is he gonna steal the cat's affection from me as well?

"Brian's allergic," Stella said.

"I know. He's been on antihistamines since he moved in with me and Mabel, my fat, furry tabby.

Good. I hope they don't work and he breaks out in hives.

She lifted the teapot. Nigel had made quick work of his first cup of tea and his cookies while stroking Mr. Velvet. "Another cup?"

"Please." He pushed his cup and saucer towards her and helped himself to three more shortbreads, leaving one for Stella.

Mr. Velvet was giving Nigel a kiss in thanks for a vigorous head and back rub while being told what a handsome boy he was.

Gigolos, the pair of them! Stella poured more tea as the animal curled up on Nigel's lap and purred himself into a snooze.

Quit being so mean. This man may have stolen your lover, but you can't help who you fall in love with. And his brother's just died.

"The reason I'm here," Nigel ventured in between shortbreads, "is because I got a call from the Los Angeles police. They had my brother's wallet with his driver's license that a garbage collector had found in a trash can, along with his backpack. They called me because it's actually my backpack I used in college, and had my name, address and telephone number stenciled on the inside. I'd lent it to Neville since he was planning a trip around the world during his gap year of graduating from high school and going to university. He's actually my half-brother. We share the same father, different mothers. My mother died when I was seven.

"I'm sorry."

Nigel paused as he finished his cookies and downed the cup of tea.

"Neville had been sending postcards as he traveled across America. The last one was sent from here, Venice. When I mentioned this to the police they asked me to...." He stopped speaking for a moment and cleared his throat. "They said a body had been found, that they thought might be his and asked if I could come over and formally identify it. I wanted them to send a photograph and relevant information to the Brighton police so I didn't have to make what might turn out to be a wasted journey, but they said, no, the body had been in the water too long, the fingerprints were corrupted. Besides, if it was Neville, and they were leaning towards certainty rather than not, there were burial arrangements to consider. When I consulted the Brighton police they agreed with the LAPD."

Stella started feeling light-headed. *I have a horrible feeling I know which dead body he's referring to.*

"Two detectives met me at the plane and drove directly to the medical examiner's office." He shuddered. "It was bad, but I knew it was him." Nigel stroked Mr. Velvet's back. "Neville was only nineteen."

"I'm so sorry. How did he die?"

"They think he drowned while swimming."

The two of them sat in silence with their own thoughts for a while, then Nigel spoke again.

"Um, Stella. Any chance of another cup of tea?"

He's probably dehydrated from the flight, not to mention shock.

"I'll have to nip next door to the grocery mart for more milk."

"I'll just sit here and wait if you don't mind." Nigel looked down at the now-sleeping cat.

"I won't be long." *Might as well get another packet of biscuits while I'm at it.*

She noticed the Snake and Parrot couple weren't at their usual station on the Boardwalk as she opened the front gate and walked to the grocery mart.

"Any news about the missing reptile?" she inquired. Mr. Patel was in his usual position at the cash register.

"No, not yet," he answered "Although I don't know why anyone would want to keep an animal like that in a modern metropolis like Los Angeles."

"I've checked everywhere around here, and in the store room," Mr. Patel continued.

"Did you look in your freezer?"

"Snakes like somewhere warm," Mr. Patel said. Then he frowned and walked over to check out his ice cream and frozen fruit bars ice chest, breathing a sigh of relief as he finished sorting through It's-It and Klondike bars. "Just in case," he explained.

In a sudden flash of caution, Stella briefly scanned behind the rows of dairy and soft drinks in the refrigerated unit before reaching in for a quart of milk. Just in case.

"You've been in here before," Mr. Patel noted as he rang up her milk and another packet of Lorna Doon shortbread. "Are you staying somewhere nearby?"

"Yes, next door, at my aunt's apartment."

"Some of the residents come in here occasionally. Who's your aunt?" Mr. Patel took the ten-dollar bill Stella handed him and gave her back the change.

"Barbara Smith."

"Ah, yes, nice lady. She's always running out of milk for her tea. Is that why she sent you on the errand this time?" He placed her purchases in a brown paper bag.

Gently, she explained to him that her aunt had died. He seemed genuinely sorry, offering his condolences as he added a couple of oranges to the bag before handing it to her.

"Don't eat too many cookies at once."

Stella thanked him and left the shop. She was on her way back to the apartment, had reached the top of the stairs and was entering the kitchen, when she heard singing.

"Baa, Baa black sheep have you any wool? Yessir, yessir, three bags full."

Nigel was on the phone with his back to the kitchen and hadn't heard her come in. "Oh, not that one? Then how about, *'I'm a poor little lamb who's lost its way. Baa-a, baa-a, baa-a,'"* he crooned, then stopped and listened to whoever was on the other end of the phone for a moment as Stella stood frozen on the spot.

What the hell was this?

"No, Brian, I'm the naughty sheep this time and you're Bo-Peep," Nigel continued. "You're supposed to chastise me with your crook. What're you wearing by the way, a Dirndl?"

Bloody cheek! Stella put her purchases down on the kitchen counter and walked into the dining-room. "What the hell are you doing singing nursery rhymes and pub songs on an expensive long-distance phone call that you think I will pay for!" *And to my ex-boyfriend that you stole!* Her sympathy meter had swung into a red zone.

Nigel jumped. "No, no, I'll pay for the call. I just phoned Brian to update him and say I'd run into you. He's been worried."

"Did Little Bo-Peep get his anxieties calmed down?"

"It's reverse psychology."

"Rubbish! It's phone sex!" Stella grabbed the phone receiver from Nigel and slammed it down.

"He needs to talk to you, Stella."

"I don't care what *he* needs. *I* don't *want* to talk to him."

"I'd promised before I left England I'd keep him updated on my situation."

Was he pleading with her? "Look, I'm sorry for your loss, but I've had losses myself lately and have enough to deal with. Brian will just have to wait his turn. He's no longer the priority on my list."

"Don't you think you're being rather childish?"

Stella's sympathy meter plummeted to zero. "Not at all."

She picked up Nigel's backpack, shoved it at his chest, then pointed to the back door.

"Goodbye. They serve pizza by the slice next door if you're hungry."

Mr. Velvet's eyes followed Nigel out the back door. He looked at Stella through slit eyes as she sat down, poured herself a cup of tea, topped it off with milk, then dunked the last shortbread from the plate before taking a bite and addressing him.

"Mr. Velvet, you're a whore cat."

CHAPTER 16

Why did Nigel have to turn up just as she was starting to feel like she was getting a grip on things? It was unnerving. As soon as she solved one problem, another one appeared. At least Nigel's presence solved one thing —the body by the rocks had been identified. It had a name. It was being taken care of. It had nothing to do with her. Nigel would deal with it and go back to England. Problem solved. Except now she felt guilty. She'd lashed out. It wasn't Nigel's fault. It wasn't hers, either. It was circumstances. Her world had been upended. So had his.

Stella, get a grip. Stop talking to yourself. She sat up straighter, finished her tea and went to look for the papers between her aunt and Bill Craven regarding *Billy's.*

There was nothing in the filing cabinet. Stella frowned. *This wasn't like Aunt Barb; she was more meticulous with business things.* She rifled through a few more files. *Nada.*

Stella reached for the phone and called Mr. Bernstein.

"Of course I have a copy of the sales agreement," he assured her. Barbara gave me one when we did her will. I asked her for a copy of everything and as far as I know, that's what I got. I'm rather surprised there isn't a copy in her files."

"Do you have a copy of her old will?"

"What old will?"

"The one I'd mentioned at our first meeting, drawn up by another law firm with some charity as executor."

"Ah, the will she'd mentioned which was moot because she'd changed her mind?"

"Right."

"No, I don't have a copy, but the current one supersedes it so moot is moot. I'd be happy to give you a copy of the final sales agreement if you feel need it. I know Barb doesn't have a fax machine, but I can have my secretary mail a copy to you. Unless you want to come by and pick one up," he added.

Stella thought about it. "When?"

"Let me check my calendar."

Stella heard paper rustling.

"How about tomorrow? Ten a.m."

"All right."

"See you then."

After they hung up, Stella checked her watch. *Too bad it hadn't been today.* She reflected back on her encounter with Nigel. He was right about one thing; she should get in touch with Brian. She felt mollified by the fact he was worried about her. It was the appropriate response. Phoning him up and actually speaking to him was out of the question. *I really don't feel like talking to him yet.*

Washing up the teacups she hit upon an idea. *I'll send him a postcard!*

Stella grabbed her bag and headed for the Boardwalk. If she ran into Nigel, she'd apologize and try to be more sympathetic. But Nigel seemed to have vanished into thin air.

Just as well. Outside a souvenir shop, Stella twirled a carousel of postcards and selected two. One would be for the office back home. Some people had looked a little too relieved when they'd not been the ones laid off. There'd been an audible sigh of relief from one or two personnel who'd not had a pink slip in their pay packet when those who had were packing up their desks and being escorted out.

Stella added a pen to her purchases and asked the storekeeper where the post office was.

"Just a couple of blocks from here, easy walking distance," he smiled and pointed in the direction before handing her some change.

After waiting in line for airmail stamps inside the small Spanish-style building at Pacific and Main, Stella stopped at a counter off to one side where people could fill out forms or place stamps on their envelopes.

"Guess where I am!' she wrote on a medley of small colorful scenes with 'Venice Beach in Sunny California' scrawled across them for the office. She smiled to herself, imagining the looks on their faces as they read it.

The postcard she'd chosen for Brian was completely black, with an inscription in the bottom corner: 'Venice by Night.'

"I'm stopping here for a while," she wrote on the back. "You can have the furniture. Send the rest of my things to my mother's house."

Done. Stella stuck the stamps on and dropped the postcards into the mailbox. She'd communicated.

On her walk back to *Billy's* Stella stopped to watch a chainsaw juggling contest by two tanned and well-muscled young men on roller skates wearing tight short-shorts. A crowd had gathered around them on the Boardwalk, laughing as pieces of watermelon, cantaloupe, oranges and apples flew through the air. Stella started laughing, too. What fun! What danger! She glanced at some of the people enjoying the show from sidewalk tables at a nearby café.

The man Stella had seen arguing with Liz near the Venice Canals was watching the jugglers. He wasn't arguing with anyone now. He was sitting with Andrea and they looked very cozy together. Food poisoning hadn't affected her, it seemed. Or, at least, she hadn't complained about it to anyone at the apartment building. *Too busy romancing every man she could get her hands on.*

Stella thought about the neighbors as she walked back to the apartment when the show had finished, starting with Gary Edwards. He might seem a bit crazy, but really he was just an individual. America liked individuality, or liked to say it did. The rest of the world just dismissed such individuality as "crazy Americans." Stella thought the difference between Americans and the English was that Americans wanted their own way. If they didn't like the system, they changed it. Brits didn't do that. If you were British you tried to fit into the system, changed yourself to fit in. *And here I am, stuck in the middle. Brainwashed Brit dealing with free-wheeling Yanks. No wonder I feel off balance.*

She thought of Andrea. So what if she wanted to conduct her life without wearing knickers? If the men in her constellation wanted to complain, Stella had no doubt they'd speak up. So far, the man on the bike, the one at the café and Sam downstairs had all seemed pretty happy. Stella wondered about the husband. Maybe that was a different story.

Liz hadn't seemed too happy with Andrea at the post-funeral party. Carol had mentioned that Liz and Sam had once dated. Perhaps Liz wasn't quite over him yet. Stella wondered about the guy watching the chain-sawing fruit exhibition. He'd seemed enamored of Andrea. Perhaps the scene she'd witnessed at the Venice Canals had been more than a lover's tiff; perhaps it had been him and Liz breaking up. Stella's mind wandered back to Gary. He'd definitely been making goo-goo eyes at Liz at the party and looked like he was in love with her. It was like the children's game of musical chairs, only this game was with adults bed-swapping their emotions.

Brian and Nigel drifted into her thoughts. Brits and Americans weren't so different on some things. People were just people when it came down to it.

The apartment building was quiet when Stella got back. No-one was home, including Carol. After microwaving left-over chicken and vegetables for dinner, which she shared with Mr. Velvet, Stella fished a business card out of her shoulder bag, picked up the phone and dialed Olivia.

"So glad you're feeling better. I'm still on a high from my art show," Olivia told her. "Would you like to come and visit my studio?"

Stella explained she would be in Beverly Hills in the morning.

"Perfect! You'd be halfway here. Almost. Why don't you come for lunch?"

She gave Stella directions, which involved getting back on the 10 freeway towards Downtown after her appointment, "then follow the signs through the crazy eight freeway changes onto the Hollywood freeway, off at Echo Park Avenue all the way up into the hills. Turn right when you reach the school for a couple of blocks, then the road wiggles left. Turn right on Valley View."

CHAPTER 17

How could a city that was so spread out be such a traffic nightmare, Stella thought, inching her way slowly forward onto the one-lane entry for the Hollywood freeway after the quick visit to Mr. Bernstein. He was busy but had still offered her coffee and biscuits as his secretary assembled the documents. *So civilized.*

Olivia's directions had seemed clear and accurate when Stella had written them down, but turning onto an uphill dirt track after consulting her notes, doubt set in. She was in the middle of a huge metropolitan city; was this the right road? There were two houses to her left, and nothing but trees and bushes on her right. Some sort of woods. Wild-looking woods.

"I'm on a county road, which means it's unpaved, at the back of Elysian Park," Olivia had said.

More like on the edge of a cliff. Stella parked at the top of the incline next to a brown-shingled house with mature eucalyptus trees all around and a goldfish pond next to a Saltillo-tiled walkway. It reminded her of the goldfish pond on *Billy's* patio. *Maybe it's an LA thing if you can't afford a swimming pool or don't have room for one.*

"The living-room's my own art gallery," Olivia explained, slowly leading her through a two-story room with vibrant paintings covering all four walls. She stopped to point out a few. "This one's from my *Sunset Boulevard* series."

Stella stared at the ink and watercolor painting. "As I mentioned when we first met, I don't know much about art."

Olivia was only too happy to enlighten her. "I'm constantly driving along the Downtown end of Sunset to get to places, including a local art school where I teach two days a week."

Stella looked more closely. It did look like part of a car. She could see a steering wheel. "Is that a coffee cup in a holder by the dashboard?"

"Yes. It's an inner/outer thing from my perspective. It's the view I see from the inside of my car while I'm driving–the buildings outside the windows, and the palm trees up on the hills."

"Ahh." Stella thought she'd got it. "The colors around the car, or that shape which you intend to represent as a vehicle, are deeper in color than the more pastel view you've depicted inside the interior looking out."

"That's right." Olivia beamed.

"You've got a beautiful home." Stella gazed around, noticing a spiral staircase in one corner.

"Thank you. That staircase goes to the loft, which is the guest bedroom. My bedroom," Olivia indicated some double glass-pained doors to the right of a fireplace which led into another room with more double doors on one wall, "leads out onto the deck."

Two large dogs of indeterminate breed lay on the deck snoozing in the sun, but raised their heads to give Stella the once-over, then lay back down and shut their eyes again.

"That's Fred and Ginger. The deck is their domain. They keep an eye on what's going on down the hill from there. My studio's through here."

Olivia led the way through a narrow kitchen to a room at the back with enormous picture windows and more French doors leading onto a small brick patio with a wrought iron table and chairs. *Lots of entrances and exits here, too, similar to Billy's.*

Olivia had a desk by one of the picture windows looking out across the hills and the Interstate 5 freeway far, far below, snaking through neighborhoods and industrial sites alongside railway lines and the concrete-entombed Los Angeles river.

"It's like an eyrie up here!" Stella was impressed. She hadn't expected Los Angeles to be so beautiful, but it was. At least what she'd seen so far. Lots of concrete to be certain, but also masses of trees and greenery.

"It's beautiful at night," Olivia conceded, "with all the headlights from freeway traffic and the twinkling lights in the hills. This is what I'm working on now."

She walked over to a large wooden easel with a drying canvas on it depicting three shadowy images of a woman with her back to the viewer, one arm posed over her shoulder as she turned to face the audience, her jeans down around her ankles showing a bare torso.

"This is my *Homage to Lynda Benglis. S*he was a woman artist who got fed up with male artists' depiction of the female nude and posed like this for the cover of *Art Forum.*"

"So she mooned the camera." Stella liked the vibrant colors and the gold leaf etching around the figures depicting a gold frame.

"The whole male-centric art world!" Olivia laughed." She took back her power. It was during the time of the Women's Movement. This is my interpretation of what she's stating: 'This is my beautiful body and I'll decide what to do with it and how it looks.'"

Stella smiled. With that kind of attitude floating around no wonder Aunt Barb had decided to stay in America. She liked Olivia, who was about her own age very bubbly, warm and friendly.

"I'm on a diet, so I made us a Cobb salad for lunch."

"Lovely."

They sat at the wrought iron table and chairs on the patio, a low but steady freeway hum in the background which had not been apparent inside the house.

"It's white noise to me now," Olivia explained as they ate. "I bought this place for the land–it's a double lot which had a wooden cabin on it at the time. My grandmother left me a small inheritance which I used as the down payment. After a while I was able to get a bank loan because of my teaching job and built the house up around the original cabin. I love it up here. There's a trail around the mountain in the park opposite and I jog with the dogs almost every day. We just got back shortly before you arrived."

No wonder they didn't bark at me; they were tired out.

Comparing the mountain park scenery to the gentle green slopes of the South Downs Stella was used to hiking, it looked like the wild west images she'd had seen in films: hot, dry and dusty. She wondered about safety up here for a woman living on her own.

"My neighbors are within shouting distance, and then there's Fred and Ginger," Olivia pointed out.

As if on cue, the dogs suddenly woke up from their nap and started barking like the Hounds of the Baskervilles.

Olivia looked at her watch. "It's the mailman. He usually comes around this time. That's why the dogs are out on the deck, otherwise I wouldn't get any mail delivered."

The dogs stopped barking and Stella heard a vehicle driving back down the hill.

"How long are you going to be in LA?"

Stella shrugged. "No idea. I have to deal with my aunt's belongings." She explained the situation starting with her aunt's invitation during the birthday phone call to her sudden decision that she might as well take her up on the vacation offer *right now*, and then the discovery of finding her aunt dead at the bottom of the stairs less than an hour after arriving in California.

"Ohmigod!" Olivia's face was a mixture of horror and sympathy. "That's a helluva start to a vacation. She suffered a slip and fall?"

"The medical examiner ruled it an accident. The police thought so, too. I'd just come from the coroner's office when I wandered into the art gallery."

"And I thought you were just a tourist exploring LA." Olivia looked at her intently. "Do I detect a note of doubt in there somewhere?"

Stella shrugged. "Then I got food poisoning at the funeral after-party."

"Jeez, no wonder you said you didn't feel well on the phone! That's like adding insult to injury. What caused it?"

"Don't know. I wasn't the only one. Some others felt unwell, but nobody's complained that they've been seriously ill. Seems that people put it down to drinking too much in the end." Stella swallowed a bite of salad. "Fortunately, my aunt has a lawyer who's been a great help. Aunt Barb appointed him executor so he's dealing with things and giving me advice. It's just a matter of time until I decide what to do, when to leave, you know."

Olivia nodded. "Well, I hope you stay much longer." She told Stella about her large family in East LA. "My mother's always criticizing what I do. She hated my ex-husband, who came from a devout Presbyterian family on the east coast. She threw a party for me when I told her we were getting a divorce. I bless my grandmother's small inheritance every day. It allowed me to build this sanctuary."

Stella felt herself relax. It felt good to let go of her anxieties as they shared personal stories; Olivia was so easy to talk to. It felt comfortable sitting in the dappled sunlight under a leafy acacia tree drinking Mexican coffee after the salad. She needed a friend, even if it was for a short time. *Billy's* tenants were friendly, too, but Stella felt less forthcoming, a little wary with them for some reason she could not fully explain. *Probably because Aunt Barb was their landlady.* She did offer up some anecdotes about the occupants and their goings-on since her arrival, but omitted Nigel's impromptu visit or any mention of Brian. Recent boyfriend break-ups had been briefly discussed at the art gallery when Olivia had been curating her own show.

Before they knew it, mid-morning had given way to late afternoon.

"I'd ask you to stay for dinner, but I'm teaching a drawing class this evening."

As if on cue, a soft bark came from the deck. Somebody had heard the word "dinner."

"I should get going anyway to try and beat some of the commuter traffic".

"Good luck on that one. It's commuter traffic 24/7 in this town."

"My aunt's cat needs feeding, too."

"Pets do require a certain amount of consideration and attention."

"It's been lovely spending time with you," Stella said as they carried the empty plates and coffee cups into the kitchen and placed them in the sink. "Why don't you come down to the beach and visit me soon, have lunch?"

"I will." Olivia opened the freezer door to her refrigerator, pulling out a container of soup and placing it on the kitchen counter to thaw. "My dinner after class," she explained.

But Stella had seen something else in the freezer compartment. *Was that a snake curled up in there, wrapped in a plastic baggie?*

Olivia noticed the look on her face. "Oh, that's my rattlesnake."

Stella gave the standard polite English response when stymied: "I see."

Don't snakes live in places like Arizona and Texas? She thought of the Snake and Parrot's missing python on the lam at the Venice Boardwalk. *Is snake ownership, alive or dead, some kind of LA fad?*

"Don't worry, it's dead. My brother lives on a ranch. He brought it to me as he knew I needed a snakeskin for one of my projects," Olivia explained as they walked back through the living-room. Her dogs had their noses pressed against the French doors. "But he didn't skin it. That's why it's in the freezer. I'm waiting for his next visit."

Stella's imagination was blank as they walked through the front door to her car. "Then what?"

"Then I can cure it."

"Cure it of what?"

"Make the skin pliable so I can use it in a painting. My brother says any vegetable oil will do, but I'm thinking Mary Kay hand lotion rather than Wesson oil. I think it'll make it softer. And maybe it will smell better."

"I see." But, she didn't.

As she slowly drove off down the dusty track avoiding any potholes, Stella thought about her short time in America: The dead body of her relative greeting her upon arrival; the silhouette of Gary Edwards aka The Peeping Tom next door in his surgeon's gown and chainsaw birthing a new surfboard; elderly albino sisters smacking each other as they argued over trash cans; the warbling bicycle duo with philandering Andrea sans panties; her aunt's cat who hangs out in a pine tree, on the beach at night, and God-knew-where-else in the neighborhood; a boutique gift shop at the Coroner's office where sobbing relatives could console themselves with a t-shirt; her relative's funeral at sea complete with self-fueled fireworks; the post-funeral party where Stella got violent food poisoning; a second post-funeral party on the beach with witches; another dead body on the rocks with her ex-lover's new lover turning up from the UK to claim it; and now Olivia's dead rattlesnake in her freezer awaiting it's next incarnation as an art project. Stella reflected back to the quiet life and little house overlooking the South Downs that she'd left behind.

I'm a stranger in a strange land.

What could possibly happen next?

CHAPTER 18

Stella drove very carefully back to the apartment after observing a car crash on the freeway when the driver of a not-so-late model vehicle in the far left lane suddenly decided he needed the off-ramp to his right *tout de suite*, pulling out and exiting across three lanes leaving a concertina-ed Volkswagen dripping gasoline and radiator water in its wake. She parked on the unauthorized lot next to Carol's truck just as Mr. Velvet came strolling down Speedway. Twilight had set in and the street lights were turning on.

"Walk with me," she said to him as they regarded each other. He followed her up the stairs and into the apartment after she unlocked the front door, "We're having fish for dinner." Stella placed her bag on the dining table. "And...," Mr. Velvet watched as she firmly shut the dining-room window, "we're having a quiet, at-home evening. An evening of reading." Stella intended to resume exploring Auntie Barb's diaries.

She went into the kitchen and opened a can of tuna, placing half in Mr. Velvet's dish and reserving the rest for her tuna sandwich, when there was a knock at the back door.

Carol stood there. "They've found a dead body on the beach," she announced as Stella unlocked and opened the door.

"What?"

"Right in front of *Billy's.*"

Stella started feeling uneasy.

"A jogger found it," Carol informed her as they walked through the garden to the front. "He'd stopped for a rest, then discovered that what he thought was soft sand under his Reeboks was actually someone's fingers poking through; the rest of the body was buried below."

"When was this?" Everything had been quiet when Stella had left that morning.

"Around noon." I came home for lunch and was at the grocery mart getting ice cream for dessert when the sound of screaming caught everyone's attention. The jogger was doing a strange little dance up and down on the sand. I thought maybe he'd found the python. Pretty soon the lifeguard truck and the ATV cops came flying across the beach, and patrol cars arrived soon after. I had to go back to work, but as you can see, they're still processing the scene."

A few neighbors were clustered around *Billy's* fence gazing across the Boardwalk. There was speculation amongst them that it was probably one of the homeless who'd been sleeping on the beach. Fights, drunken or otherwise, broke out from time to time and now and then someone overdosed. It was the dark side of paradise.

Police tape cordoned off a wide area around some wooden telegraph poles which had been cut down to different heights and arranged in the sand so children could play on them or people could sit down. Unmarked police cars were parked alongside patrol cars on the bike path and detectives were combing the area, while uniformed officers held back small groups of people who, on their evening walk, had stopped to watch. Other cops were setting up spotlights around the scene.

"The detectives haven't been here long," said the woman who'd worn her small dog in a baby sling across her chest at Aunt Barb's after funeral party. "And neither have the crime scene techs. Must've been a busy day in the Big Bad City. I mean, there's only so many personnel to go around, what with all the latest budget cuts."

Stella remembered her name was Cindy. She wasn't wearing her dog now. It was snuffling around the yard, nose down. Every now and then it lifted its leg against a plant pot.

"Percy! Cut that out! You little stinker!" Cindy tried to pick him up, but he dodged her. "You little shit! Come here!" She finally grabbed him.

So much for motherly love.

"He's a cute little poodle," Stella offered, smiling at the two beady eyes barely visible though Percy's mop of hair.

"He's not a poodle, he's a p'doodle," Cindy amended. "A cross between a Pomeranian and a poodle."

Okay, a classic mutt. Whatever. "He's still cute."

"Just don't get between him and his food."

"Wouldn't dream of it." Stella turned her attention back to the crime scene.

"They're bagging the hands now." Gary Edwards stood by his fence next door staring through what looked like circa World War II military binoculars.

"Greg's got the best view," Carol remarked, turning her gaze upwards to where he gazed down on everything from his front window.

The picture-postcard beach scenes Stella had mailed yesterday were turning into a live danger zone.

I'm gonna sell this building.

"Here comes the Coroner's van," Gary announced lowering his binoculars as a black vehicle came down Brooks Avenue and lumbered onto the Boardwalk. It stopped in front of *Billy's*, blocking their view. Everyone shifted further down the fence toward Gary as the driver and his assistant opened the back doors and pulled out a gurney.

Oh, great! From her new position Stella recognized one of the police officers searching the sand. He'd been at the apartments the night she'd arrived and found her aunt near the bottom of the stairs. They'd met again when Nigel's brother, Neville, had been discovered wedged in seaweed on the rocks. What had he said to her then as he'd tapped his note book and mentioned that he knew where to find her if he had to? *Try not to find any more dead bodies or I'll start to get suspicious.* She hadn't known whether he was teasing her or being serious at the time. Now here they were again. Another dead body. Just an innocent coincidence, but it didn't do to be on the radar of a policeman in a foreign country.

I might be suspicious of me, too, Stella reasoned to herself, inadvertently stepping back into the shadows before he could spot her. She'd watched enough television police shows where someone had remarked that the perpetrator would often be an observer in the crowd. This whole thing was making her feel uncomfortable, even though she had nothing to do with it. She turned to go back inside.

"They're loading the body onto the gurney." Gary Edwards was rapidly adjusting his binoculars. "I think it's a woman!"

Stella couldn't help it. She had to look. Things were happening that she'd never seen before and probably never would again. *Most people would go to Disneyland on their vacation.* Obviously, the gods had had other ideas for her.

"Omigod!" Gary Edwards' jaw dropped. "It's Andrea!"

There was a collective indrawn breath among the neighbors as they strained forward for a better look as she was zipped into a body bag.

"No!"

"Damn!"

"How did that happen?"

They started speculating amongst themselves again. Who had last seen her? When? Who with? Did she OD while sunbathing?

"Where's Sam?"

Stella looked around. He wasn't there. Probably at work. Liz wasn't there, either, but she usually worked an evening waitress shift. Stella glanced up at Greg's window. He'd disappeared.

CHAPTER 19

Stella made sure the front and back doors were securely locked before going to bed that night. *Forget reading.* She had trouble concentrating on anything and didn't even bother to make her tuna sandwich, let alone eat it. All the tenants were upset and had tried to console each other after the Coroner's van left. The police wouldn't give them any information.

Mr. Velvet jumped on the Murphy bed and curled up by Stella's feet as she pulled the covers up close. Soon, they were both asleep. Stella dreamed she was being chased by someone she couldn't see. She kept looking back as she fled, but there was only a silhouette running after her; the assailant was too far away to discern any features.

At the foot of the bed, Mr. Velvet lay dreaming, too. His paws twitched and he emitted a low growl now and then. But he was the hunter in his dream, after a bird that he couldn't catch. A seagull who taunted him kept hopping out of range with mocking cries and was joined by several others that dive-bombed him repeatedly, driving him off.

Both dreamers woke up still tired and yawning. As Stella stumbled towards the bathroom she spied a note someone had slipped under the front door. She picked it up and unfolded it. *Sorry,* she read. It was signed, Nigel. Attached was a $20 bill for the transatlantic phone call. Stella felt guilty and resolved to be nicer to him if they ever met up again.

Mr. Velvet was sitting by the dining room window. As Stella went to open it a woman wearing a loose house dress that looked suspiciously like a nightie came out of the Edwards' house and walked across the yard. She had long white hair that lifted behind her in the morning breeze like a ship in full sail. Stopping in front of a bed of Cosmos she suddenly flapped her arms, then waggled her fingers.

Was this some sort of ritual to help the flowers grow? Stella wondered, then noticed the bright red fingertips. The woman was merely drying her nail polish; probably her hair, too. At least Stella hoped she was. This must be Gary's mother. Maybe a mad mother? Stella hoped not, but nothing would surprise her any more. Carol had told her Mrs. Edwards had been ill recently.

The shrill whistle of a tea kettle invaded the yard from the open kitchen door.

"Oops, gotta go," the old lady told the flowers and gave them a last wave goodbye before disappearing indoors.

Mr. Velvet had been watching intently and as soon as Stella opened the window he jumped onto a tree branch, ran down the trunk and over to the flower bed where he dug a hole and squatted.

"Oh, bad boy," Stella muttered under her breath, wondering if Gary and his mother knew about the organic fertilizer helping their flowers bloom so prettily.

While Mr. Velvet took care of his morning ablutions, Stella noticed small finches darting around a bird feeder on a branch hanging over the driveway. One bird was flying back and forth between the tree and the fence on the far side of the Edwards's yard. *That's odd.* Half-hidden by some overgrown bushes the fence had some weird things hanging on it: a dilapidated lifeguard ring from the *S.S. Rex;* a number of children's buckets and spades, some rusty; various parts of kids' broken toys.

Stella frowned. Was that little bird ripping out hair from a Barbie doll head? She followed the finch's flight back to the nest it was building on a flimsy upper branch of the pine tree, silvery blonde synthetic strands streaming from its beak. She watched it fuss with the pale strands, patting them into place, and marveled at nature's adaption and ability to make things up as it went along. Moment to moment. That's all any of us have when it comes down to it, Stella thought sadly, remembering Andrea's lust for life. Still, who would hang Barbie on a fence?

Someone was knocking at her front door. "Come in, Carol," Stella said as she opened it.

Mr. Velvet was back in the tree, his teeth chattering at the finch whose nest was too high up amongst more slender branches for him to reach.

"Look at this," Stella pointed across the Edwards' yard.

"That's Gary's trophy fence." Carol was dismissive. "He picks up any flotsam and jetsam washed ashore that he finds interesting. I put it down to some weird male way of decorating."

Stella put aside any unnerving thoughts about middle-aged men who lived with their mothers as Carol continued.

"Listen, the police took Sam in for questioning after you came back to the apartment last night. He's still down at the police station."

The sound of a vehicle parking outside on Speedway and men's loud voices entering the building floated up from downstairs. Keys rattled.

Carol re-opened Stella's door and peeked out. "That's them, the cops. They're searching his apartment. You might want to get dressed in case they come up here."

Stella panicked. "Why would they do that?"

"Because it's your aunt's building."

"But she's dead."

"You're her representative."

"Shit!"

"Get dressed!"

Stella grabbed some clothes and went into the bathroom to change, while Carol tidied the bed for her, shoving it back into the wall before opening the window blinds in the back room. They could hear the police moving about in the apartments below; first Sam's, then Andrea's.

"I need fortification." Stella was wide awake now she'd brushed her teeth and combed her hair. She put the kettle on. Mr. Velvet sat by his dish waiting for a Kitty Kibbles replenishment, which Stella gave him, then opened the kitchen door so he could go out when he was done eating.

"Have you had breakfast yet?" she asked Carol who'd sat down at the dining-table.

"No." Carol shook her head.

Just as Stella was fixing a pot of tea and about to put it on the table, there was a knock at the door.

"Cops," Carol mouthed.

Stella grimaced and didn't move. She stood stock still, clutching the teapot for dear life. There was another knock, louder this time. Carol raised her eyebrows at Stella who indicated she should go ahead and open the door.

"Ah, Ms. Maris." Her nemesis stood on the threshold looking past Carol at Stella. "Can we come in?"

She managed a nod and Carol opened the door wider. Officer Martinez and his partner stepped in. The room seemed now seemed overcrowded to Stella, who was feeling nervous for absolutely no reason that she could pinpoint other than she was totally out of her depth ever since she'd landed in this bloody town. No, before that; since she'd boarded the first plane at Gatwick.

She indicated the teapot. "Would you like a cup of tea?"

The two cops stared at her with amusement, then at each other, then back at her.

"Ms. Maris, this isn't a social call."

Stella felt indignant. "Well, it's what we do in England." *But you're not getting cookies.*

Officer Martinez smiled. "Yes, we've seen those British cop shows on PBS. Very civilized."

Is he smirking?

"Would you like to sit down, officers?"

"We're not staying long." Martinez placed his business card on the table and Baker did the same. "We just have a couple of questions about the tenants downstairs. Either of you notice anything strange going on? Anything out of the ordinary?"

Stella stifled a laugh and put the teapot down. "I've only been here a short while. This is my aunt's place; she can't tell you anything because she's dead. I know nothing about anybody. Frankly, this place and everything that's happened since I arrived is every shade of strange."

She knew she was being unfair, but she couldn't help herself. None of the things happening was America's fault, but it really was all too much. She felt like blaming somebody. Or something. Maybe Nigel was right. Some sort of childishness was creeping in. Her mother was right, too. Stella could handle it. She poured herself a cup of tea.

Sergeant Martinez turned to Carol. "How about you?"

"Sam moved in a little less than a year ago. Andrea moved in about four months ago. They both seemed like nice young people. Barbara liked them, otherwise she wouldn't have rented to either of them."

"What's the story about the doorway in their adjoining closets?"

Carol shrugged. "They liked each other?"

Now it was Officer Baker's turn to adopt the shadow of a smirk.

"How did she die?" Stella felt compelled to ask; her uneasy feeling was not going away. In fact, it was getting stronger. *Three* dead bodies? Okay, so two were accidents. Supposedly, although how could she be so sure now? Two of the bodies were connected to *Billy's* in some way.

"We have to wait for the autopsy results," Martinez told them. "We'll let you know." He turned to leave. "In the meantime," he pointed to their business cards on the table. "Give us a call if you think of anything."

Carol closed the door behind them as they clomped down the stairs.

"Thank you," Stella told her. "I'm absolutely out of my depth here. Would you like a cup of tea?"

"No thanks, I've already had coffee and I have to get to work." She hesitated, remembering something. "The rent's due in a couple of days. Are there any changes? Do we still pay it straight into Barbara's bank account? You haven't said anything and we don't know what's going on."

"Join the club. Things are still being sorted out. Just carry on doing what you normally do. Can't give you any answers at the moment, I'm afraid." In light of this new occurrence with Andrea perhaps it was a good thing she hadn't confided in any of the tenants.

Carol nodded. "All right. For what it's worth, none of us think Sam had anything to do with Andrea's death."

"Good to know." Stella had a sudden thought. "By any chance, do you know who her husband is? Was? Is? Has anyone ever met him?"

Carol shook her head. "No idea. I don't think he ever came round here. If he did, I never met him. No one else has ever mentioned ever meeting him."

And yet people know he exists.

"I'm sure the police will contact him. I think he lives in LA somewhere. He'll probably turn up for her stuff. And then there's a funeral or something for Andrea. Some of us would like to attend that. If I hear anything, I'll let you know."

"Okay. Thank you."

After Carol left, Stella reached for the phone and left a message for Harry Bernstein to call her back as soon as he could. Then she collected the sales contract between her aunt and Bill Craven from her bag. After the discovery of Andrea's body, she'd forgotten to put it away the night before. She'd have to check the filing cabinet again, see if there was a file of some sort to do with Craven somewhere in there. But first, a bowl of Cheerios.

She read the contract while she ate her breakfast. It was short and simple, just a couple of pages. Luckily, there was a phone number in Idaho for him jotted down in ink on the second page. She'd have to ask Bernstein if he'd called him; the lawyer hadn't mentioned it.

The phone rang. "Mr. Bernstein returning your call," a secretary's voice said.

She waited while he came on the line.

"Morning Stella. I was going to call you today, but you go first. What's up at your end?"

She told him about Andrea.

"Good God! What on earth's going on down there?"

"Don't know. It looks like a suspicious death, but what sort, I don't know. The police aren't saying anything yet." She thought about her other question. "You haven't by any chance talked to Bill Craven, have you?"

"I put in a couple of calls, and sent him a short letter, but I've yet to hear back."

"The phone number on the agreement's still good?"

"Seems so. He could be off at fish camp or something. You could try contacting him if you want."

"I'll do that." Stella made a mental note to call Bill Craven next. "What was it you wanted to call me about?"

"There's a problem with probate. Somebody's filed another will on behalf of your aunt; it's dated six days before she died."

"What!"

"The court's faxing me over a copy this morning."

Stella was non-plussed. She'd woken up worried by Andrea's death. Something was going on around here, something underhanded, something she didn't understand, and she was getting afraid. And very, very annoyed. Whatever it was, whoever it was, how dare they!

"You mentioned an old will," Mr. Bernstein reminded her, "Can you tell me what date it has?"

"Hang on," Stella replied, "I'll get it from the file."

She was back in one minute flat. "It says 'February 12, 1991.'"

"Okay, ours is dated December 16, 1992–the one that leaves everything to you. I need to see the original of that old one of yours. In the meantime, can you fax me a copy?"

Stella hesitated. "I don't have a fax machine."

"Barbara used one that they have in a little book shop on the Boardwalk, not too far from the apartment. It's next to a café. Can you do it as soon as possible? I've got appointments for the rest of the day, but if you can come by with the original tomorrow, I'll look at the copy in the meantime."

"Okay." Bill Craven would have to wait.

The book shop wasn't far. Stella faxed the will to Mr. Bernstein and paid the assistant. On her way out she stopped at a display loaded with journals and artist's sketch books. *Ah, so this is where Aunt Barb bought her little black books to write in!* There were several sizes, some even had lines. Stella bought one without. She was going to follow Aunt Barb's example, start her own little black book, write her own diary of what had happened since she'd arrived; all the goings-on. Because something was definitely going on.

As she left the book shop and walked back along the Boardwalk, Stella planned where she would start to jot things down. Right from the beginning, Day 1 and the phone call from Aunt Barb.

She didn't notice that someone was following her.

CHAPTER 20

She was about to telephone Bill Craven when there was a knock on the kitchen door, which she'd left open to let the sea breeze riffle through the apartment. A man stood there in a tee shirt, cargo shorts and a pair of flip-flops.

"Yes?" Stella didn't recognize him, although she had a feeling she might have seen him somewhere before.

"I'm looking for Barbara Smith. This is the last address I have for her."

"I'm afraid she doesn't live here any more."

He looked crestfallen. "I've come a long way to talk to her in person. I'm Ray's son, Scott."

Stella thought she detected a Canadian accent. A son, eh? She didn't remember anyone in the family ever mentioning that Auntie Barb's late husband had a child.

"I'm Barbara's niece, Stella. You better come in." She indicated a chair and he sat down at the dining-room table.

"I've come to apologize. The last time we saw each other was at my dad's funeral where we argued and exchanged some very harsh words. Did she move somewhere nearby?"

Stella took a deep breath. "My aunt died recently," she said gently.

"So, I'm too late?"

Stella shook her head sadly. "Yes."

He sighed. "I tried to write a few times, but always tore the letter up. It seemed inadequate. When my wife and I discussed bringing our boys to Disneyland for their school spring break. I thought I'd take the opportunity to drop by in person and see if we could make amends."

Now Stella remembered him; he was the dad explaining jellyfish and ocean currents to his sons when she'd taken her first walk along the beach.

"We're going back to Toronto in a couple of days. It's taken awhile for me to pluck up my courage." Scott laughed ruefully. "I could have come by sooner and saved myself some angst."

He looked around the apartment. "So you live here now? By yourself"

"At the moment."

He nodded. "I was Ray's only son."

As far as you know. Ray had been a musician, after all. He'd traveled a lot.

"My parents split up when I was a baby, but Ray kept in touch."

Stella wondered why he was really here. Scott seemed nice enough, but she hoped this wasn't going to turn into a further complication. Money was a powerful motive for all sorts of things, and Stella knew from previously working at a law firm, arguments amongst relatives at funerals was common. Lifelong vitriol emerged.

"Barbara was always nice to me on the occasions we did meet. In the end, she was more generous than my dad." He shrugged his shoulders. "I just never said thank-you."

And now it's too late.

They were both silent for a moment. Stella contemplated the word gratitude. *We don't focus on it enough in our lives.*

Scott stared out the window. "There's a cat sitting in the tree! Do you always keep this window open?"

"Yes. It's his cat door."

He laughed. "Well, I'll be darned! Here, kitty, kitty. Here."

Mr. Velvet didn't budge from his perch.

They chatted for a few more minutes, and Stella offered Scott a cup of tea, but he said he had to go. They shook hands on the back porch.

"Nice meeting you, Stella."

"Likewise." She watched him walk down the steps Greg had so recently rebuilt and through the garden before he disappeared around the front apartment building and onto the Boardwalk. It was then she realized he knew where she lived, but he hadn't given her his address.

It was a lovely sunny day, a little cooler than the day before, courtesy of a stiff breeze coming off the ocean. The garden between the building was sheltered from the wind though, and mostly quiet from any Boardwalk noise. Stella checked her watch.

"Time for a quick call to Bill Craven, and then a working lunch," Stella told Mr. Velvet, who'd jumped through the window and joined her on the porch.

There was no answer at the Idaho number. Like Auntie Barb, the man didn't have an answering machine, either. Stella hung up and went to make a tuna sandwich and a carafe of strong coffee, which she took down to the patio along with her new journal. Mr. Velvet followed closely on her heels, jumping onto the round ironwork table under the bougainvillea as Stella sat down next to him in one of the garden chairs. She fed him tidbits of tuna while contemplating what she was going to write.

She noted down timeline details and a few of her reactions. Stella had just finished jotting down a few particulars about the Hecate's Hags' celebration when Carol strolled through from the Boardwalk, a slice of pizza and a diet Coke in hand.

"Mind if I join you?" She sat down at the table. Mr. Velvet sniffed at the melted cheese.

"No way, Jose," Carol told him, taking a bite of pizza, her eyes on Stella's journal–which she quietly closed. "Keeping a travel diary?"

"Something like that."

"Heard anything more about Andrea?"

Stella shook her head. "The cops never came back, at least not yet."

"They questioned the neighbors last night," Carol said, "but no-one could tell them much. Is Sam back?"

"Not as far as I know. It's been pretty quiet. I haven't seen anybody, except I did get a glimpse of Gary's mother talking to her flowers."

"So, she's finally up and about. That's good."

"I had another visitor after you left."

Stella told Carol about Scott. "He didn't know Auntie Barb had died. You've lived here a long time and were friends with her. You knew Ray, too. Scott mentioned the friction between him and my aunt at his father's funeral."

"Friction!" Carol laughed. "More like a full-blown argument. I think he bullied her into giving him money to make him go away. At least that was my opinion. Barbara had a good heart; I think she was always nicer to Scott than his dad was. From what I gathered, father and son never got along." She swallowed the last bite of pizza with a drink of Coke. "Barbara bought this building after Ray died." She took another sip of the Coke. "Any more news on that front?"

"It's in the hands of her lawyer," Stella said. "Everything's up in the air."

Carol nodded. "I've got to get back to work." She let Mr. Velvet lick the pizza-stained paper plate, then stood up and crumpled it, along with the diet Coke can. "See you later."

Stella continued writing for a while, then stopped. Carol had mentioned Auntie Barb giving Scott money. She wondered if her aunt had written about it in her diary. Probably. But Stella didn't think that was what the Night Mother wanted her to read. It was something else.

CHAPTER 21

The next morning Stella and Mr. Bernstein poured over the three wills in his office. The old one from February 12, 1991 with the "moot" Post-it that had been attached was identical to the most recent one that had been filed dated February 12, 1993 with Gabriel Charities as executor and beneficiary, but minus the list of individual charities her aunt had attached to the 1991 will. The document Aunt Barbara had drawn up with Harry Bernstein a couple of months before her death dated December 16, 1992, with him as executor and Stella as sole beneficiary, was very different.

"February 12, 1993 was two days before my birthday, around the time Aunt Barb phoned me and a few days before I arrived and found her dead."

"I don't like this," Harry remarked. "There's something wrong about it." He reached for the phone and dialed Information for the Charities' phone number. It wasn't listed.

"No address either," Harry noted. "Could be Barbara typed up the will herself."

"She doesn't have a typewriter or word processor in the apartment," Stella said.

"Maybe a friend did it for her and she just signed it," Bernstein replied. "It's boilerplate language, looks like from a simple will book which you can get in any bookstore. They look the same, but I'm going to go over both of these line by line to make sure they are."

He turned to the back page on the documents. "The Notary Public's the same name on each one. Just a minute." Bernstein opened his desk drawer and pulled out a magnifying glass to briefly scour each one. "Ahh, I can just make out the Commission number and expiration date on the official stamp. They look the same on both documents." He put the magnifying glass down. "The only difference in these identical wills are the dates, 1991 and 1993." His mouth twitched as his gaze turned inward for a second; then he looked at Stella.

"I smell a rat. Your aunt wouldn't have gone back on her intention without telling me beforehand, I believe she wanted you to be her beneficiary. Leave this with me," he tapped the 1991 document," and we'll get it straightened out. I can't tell if the one in 1991 was changed to a three, but I think someone was very clever and very careful and did alter it. We can get an expert's opinion on that if needs be."

"There's something else."

"What?"

"A man stopped by the apartment yesterday and said he was the son of Auntie Barb's late husband, Ray. His name was Scott and he said he was on vacation with his family. Apparently, he and my aunt had exchanged some harsh words at his father's funeral and he wanted to apologize in person. He didn't know she'd died."

"Did he give you his address or phone number?"

"No."

"His last name?"

Stella shook her head. "I presume it was the same as his father – Smith."

"Hmmnn." Harry looked thoughtful. "See if you can find an address book, Barbara's or maybe an old one of Ray's."

"I didn't notice anything like that when I was looking through drawers and cupboards in the apartment originally. She seems to have kept everything in her file cabinet like that, addresses and things, and I didn't see anything of Ray's."

"She my have cleared his stuff out after he died."

"Unless there's something, an address or phone number, in her diaries."

"She kept a diary?" Harry perked up. "Take a look at that."

"There's dozens of them. She'd been keeping journals since the 1960's."

"Arrange them in order and start by looking at the last few years," he suggested. "There might be something in there that explains things."

Stella nodded and stood up to go. *It might even mention you.* "Right." *And that's both you and The Night Mother telling me what to do.*

He walked her to the elevator.

"It would be good if you can hang around a bit longer, extend your vacation. Can you do that? You might have to appear in court."

Stella thought she could hang around for a bit. After all, she'd lost her home, her boyfriend and her job, which had prompted her spontaneous vacation idea and flight to California. Too bad Auntie Barb had slipped and fallen right before she'd arrived. *If* she'd slipped and fallen. So what if it had been ruled an accident? Stella frowned again. She was now more than ever convinced that it wasn't which made her feel very uncomfortable, but resigned.

"Okay." *Might as well sort out this mess first.* After all, there was only another one waiting for her in England. And this one came with professional help. In reality as well as in her dreams.

Harry pushed the elevator button. "And be careful. The beach is lovely, but there's a lot of crazies wandering around out there."

As she waited for the elevator, Stella's mind reflected back to when she found the older will in her aunt's filing cabinet, along with the one Mr. Bernstein had drawn up, which she'd taken to her first meeting with him. When she'd returned to the beach that evening, after the harrowing incident where she'd narrowly escaped being run over, the door to her apartment had been ajar. She'd thought it was the ancient lock, dating from 1910 when the apartments were built, which had not fastened properly and needed replacing. But then the filing cabinet had been slightly open; she'd attributed that to herself not properly closing it. The old will was still inside, although the Post-it had been on the floor. Nobody seemed to have been in the apartment. Or had they? Stella frowned. What were they after, and why were they after her? If they really were after her. She couldn't shake the feeling that they were.

Her aunt had taken Harry Bernstein into her confidence and they'd been friends. Stella decided she'd put her confidence in him, too. She had a hunch he didn't like coincidences, either.

The "Down" elevator was taking its time, so Stella decided to make a quick pit stop. Two women, both professionally dressed, were bending over the wash basins in front of the mirror when Stella walked into the restroom. They quickly straightened up and started checking their hair and makeup.

"Best way to drop those last few pregnancy pounds I ever found," one of the women said to the other casually concealing something in her jacket pocket.

Stella walked into a stall and closed the door, but not before noticing a trace of white powder under the woman's nostrils as she'd checked her lipstick.

"Have you got those documents ready that I need," she heard one of them say as both women exited the restroom together.

"They're on your desk."

The door closed behind them.

Oh great! Stella thought to herself. *An attorney and her secretary sharing a cocaine break.* She flushed the toilet. "City of Angels be damned."

It was only three flights down, so she decided to take the stairs instead, then headed for one of the pay phones in the building lobby and dialed Olivia's number. The answering machine clicked on. *Darn it!* Stella left a brief voicemail, then headed into the parking garage, retrieved the Mercedes, and drove back to the beach.

She spread a towel near the water line, and lay down on her stomach in her bikini and one of Aunt Barb's straw hats after liberally applying sunscreen. The sun was warm on her back, kneading out any muscle tension as a light breeze from the ocean played over her bare arms and legs. *God, early spring in Southern California feels good,* she wrote in her journal, propped up on her elbows. *I could get used to this,* After jotting down facts to bring things up to date, including the visit with Harry Bernstein, she closed the journal and reached for one of Aunt Barb's diaries she'd brought along to leaf through and opened a page at random.

God I've just turned thirty and I'm still unmarried. As Stella turned a page, it seemed that Aunt Barb had just broken up with Ray. It was dated twenty years earlier.

She tossed the book aside. "Don't worry, you'll get back together again and he will marry you," she sighed out loud to no-on in particular, stretching out on the towel and closing her eyes. *Too close to home Only Brian and I won't make up and get married.* Pretty soon Stella was snoring lightly. And starting to dream.

She stood in the lobby of an office building not unlike the one at the lawyer's. The elevator door opened with a middle-aged woman tap dancing inside. She looked like what could only be described as Yankee Doodle Dandy in a red, white and blue sequined outfit that showered sparkling light over everything.

"Hi, I'm The Great Mother!" she chirped at Stella, her feet not missing a beat. "And I'm here to remind you that nothing's written in concrete, and if it is, it's still not gonna last long."

Stella's mouth opened, but The Great Mother had more to add. "So, if you think something's forever and ever, you're in big trouble. That's number one. Number two." The woman tapped a few steps and flourished her cane. "You've got to learn who people are. What you see is not always what you get. And don't let others tell you what you're looking at, either," she added. The Great Mother tapped her cheek with her cane that looked suspiciously like a wand. "Number three–what was it? Oh yes, it's time for you to pick up the pace, Stella. Come on! Wake up! Get going!"

Tap-tap-tap, tap-tap-tap. Dada-dada-da-duh! Yankee Doodle Dandy ended her dance with a flourish

Even though she was sleeping and supposedly relaxed, Stella felt annoyed. She was not in the mood for a lecture; it made her feel like she'd done something wrong. Who were these women turning up in her dreams? She started talking in her sleep.

"Are you any relation to The Night Mother? You don't look a bit like her. She wasn't blonde."

"What did I just tell you about appearances? I know who I am. It's you who doesn't know who you really are." She reached out and pressed the elevator button with her wand. "Are you coming?"

Before Stella could make up her mind, the open elevator started ascending like a swing in a high wire act.

"So, wake up, kiddo! And what else was it, let me think now. Oh, yes. Read the book! The little black book!" The Great Mother shouted down, sending sequined sparks like the tail of a comet showering over Stella.

She awoke to the screeching cry of seagulls having a fight in mid-air over a tidbit one had stolen from the other. Pretty soon others gathered and the air was filled with flapping wings and screeching cries as the bird community joined in on one side or the other. Everyone had an opinion. Stella sat up feeling hot and grumpy. A crust of bread dropped from one bird's beak and was quickly snatched up by another before the flock dispersed and flew off. The tide was going out. *I am reading those little black books! I just have to find the right one!*

Her head ached. Stella poked her arm with her finger—slightly pink. Time to go in. She reached for her dress and threw the diaries into the beach bag. She'd have to call her mother and bring her up to date. Sheila and Jim would be back in England by now. But what to say? Stella didn't want to mention her crazy dreams and she certainly wasn't going to tell her mother about two more dead bodies. The woman would panic and tell her to get on the next plane out. Which might not be a bad idea, but she'd promised Harry to stay awhile.

Olivia was standing on the back porch when she got back to *Billy's* holding a brown paper-wrapped object under her arm.

"Got your message," she said as Stella climbed the back stairs. "I was out jogging with the dogs when you called." She was smiling. "Tried calling you back, but since there was no answer I thought I'd just drive down here." She nodded at the package under her arm. "I have a present for you. After I finished painting, I decided you should have it."

Stella unlocked the back door and the two women walked into the dining room, where she unwrapped the brown paper as Olivia sat down in Mr. Velvet's armchair.

"Call it a late birthday present or a souvenir from Los Angeles that you can take back to England," Olivia said.

It was the "Homage to Lynda Benglis" painting that had been in progress when Stella visited Olivia's home and studio, her take on artist Lynda Benglis' 1970s ad in *Artforum* magazine which had challenged the male-centric art world on gender and identity. Three abstract forms of a nude woman, jeans down around her ankles, glanced back over the shoulder at the observer.

"It was controversial at the time, an answer to how female nudes had been depicted by male artists for hundreds of years," Olivia commented as Stella studied the painting etched in gold leaf which complimented the bright-hued yellow, blue and purple figures.

Stella was touched by Olivia's generosity. "I really like it. Thank you."

Olivia beamed. "Oh, goody. Are you up for an early dinner, a little stroll on the Boardwalk?'

"Absolutely. Let me just rinse off and get changed."

At that moment, Mr. Velvet came flying through the open window onto the dining table where he sat and licked his paws while eyeing Olivia sitting in his chair.

"Omigod! Does she always do that?" Olivia stared at the little black cat intently.

"Yes," Stella laughed as she propped the painting on a dining-room chair then went into the bathroom. "It's *his* cat door."

The pair of them were having a love fest when she came out.

"You're so-o beautiful," Olivia crooned, stroking Mr. Velvet under his chin as he gazed back at her in ecstasy through half-closed eyes, purring madly, the tip of his little pink tongue showing.

"He just loves to be loved." Stella walked into the back room to select a dress and heeled sandals from the closet before going into the kitchen and pouring Kitty Kibbles into his cat dish.

"Don't we all." Olivia acknowledged as Mr. Velvet abruptly broke off from her petting and headed for his dinner.

Stella turned to her friend. "Ready?" All thoughts of dreams and danger vanished from her mind.

CHAPTER 22

A smell of Givenchy and Chanel hung over the bike path as rollerbladers in their college sweatshirts and tees glided past each other in the sand-and-tan's version of cocktail hour. Some exchanged notes as they passed each other, or shouted out directions to where they'd be later. A late afternoon hockey game had started up in the nearby municipal parking lot using empty trash cans as goalposts.

"It's an outdoor gym," Olivia observed as she and Stella strolled along the Boardwalk.

"Yes, I've come to the conclusion that Los Angeles is one big work out," Stella replied as they turned the corner onto Navy Street.

"Too true." Olivia opened the glass door to Chaya Venice on the corner of Navy and Main. "Do you like sushi?"

"Never had it," Stella said glancing around the restaurant which had a few early diners and a full complement of cocktail drinkers gathered around the bar. "But I'll try anything. And, I love fish, being from a beach town myself."

"They also do American food," Olivia advised as the hostess led them to a small table.

"This is my treat, a thank-you for the painting," Stella told her as they opened their menus. "Want a cocktail?"

"How about some hot sake," Olivia answered.

Over a Deluxe Sushi Special and Sashimi Combo, two Pacific red snapper entrees, and mango mochi for dessert, Stella brought Olivia up to date on her SoCal sojourn so far.

"You mean your ex-partner's new boyfriend turned up from England to identify his brother's dead body?" Olivia was agog. Stella had told her that she'd recently broken up with Brian when they first met but hadn't gone into details. "Omigod, poor guy. Bastard, too, I mean."

Then Stella mentioned the phone sex.

"Hang on." Olivia signaled the waiter for another flagon of sake. Large. The first one had gone down well. And fast. "What a nerve! But you have to admit, he must have been very stressed out."

"I do. I felt sorry for him, but annoyed at the same time. It was very unnerving."

They discussed the Brian and Nigel situation for a while, along with lovers' betrayals in general. Then Stella told Olivia about Andrea's murder.

"Good God!" Olivia went to pour another cup of sake and realized they'd run out again already. She raised her eyebrows at Stella, who signaled the waiter for a third flagon.

"Two dead bodies in what, less than a month since you arrived?" Olivia blurted out.

"Three, if you count Aunt Barb's accident." Stella had lowered her voice and sneaked a quick glance right and left to see if anyone was listening.

Olivia frowned and lowered her voice, too. "Maybe it wasn't such an accident."

"That's what I've begun to think."

"Hmmn."

They were silent for a moment as the waiter brought the new flagon and replenished their drinks.

Olivia sipped her sake. "The thing is Stella, you're living in a public and popular place. Venice has something like 60,000 residents and 250,000 visitors walking past your apartment building on weekends. What about the neighbors?"

Stella told her about Carol next door, Liz, Cindy and Greg in the front building, and Sam and Andrea downstairs. "The police let Sam go after questioning him."

"What about the house next door?"

"Gary the middle-aged surfer lives with his elderly mother who's been ill recently. He's a bit eccentric, but doesn't strike me as a murderer, more of an individualist, if you know what I mean. From what I hear, he's a kind neighbor to Vi and Edna, the elderly women who live in the green-gabled house directly across from his on the corner of Speedway. They seem to be slowly going mad in their old age, but I don't think they have enough energy to be bumping people off, even if they are only seen outside at night.

Olivia sat up s little straighter. "Why is that?"

"They're albinos."

"How do you know if they only come out at night?"

"Carol told me one evening when they were fighting over putting out the trash cans."

"They don't sound too decrepit."

"They're in their nineties."

"My grandmother was taking care of herself until she passed at 102. And that was only because she fell off a stepladder while she was painting her kitchen ceiling. They might not be as frail as you think."

"Look, the Coroner's office ruled that Nigel's brother accidentally drowned while swimming and my aunt tripped and fell on rickety wooden stairs while watering her potted plants at night, which stairs have since been repaired by Greg. The only suspicious death is Andrea's, and we still don't know if she'd didn't die while sunbathing, even though she was covered in sand."

Olivia snorted. "Yeah, right."

Even to Stella that explanation sounded far-fetched. In her heart of hearts she knew it wasn't true. Someone had had it in for the young woman.

"As you've just pointed out, the beach and the Boardwalk are full of strangers as well as locals, so who knows? The police are still investigating." Stella downed a mouthful of sake. "Apparently, Andrea had a coterie of men on hand."

She told Olivia about the artist lover announcing his arrival as he cycled down the alley, and the back and forth bird calls between them before Andrea hopped on the back of his bike and they rode off together. "She wasn't wearing any knickers."

"Is that a valid reason to get killed?"

Both women pondered this for a moment.

"Could be," Stella finally decided.

"If she makes a habit of it."

"Men flashing their bits is a no-no, but women? Different standard," Stella pointed out. "We're a salacious society."

"Yeah, Lynda Benglis nailed it twenty years ago."

The women polished off their third flagon as their waiter approached. "Are you ladies ready for the check, yet?"

Stella glanced around. She had no idea how long they'd been sitting there, but the restaurant was filling up with more people waiting to be seated. "Guess so."

She looked across at Olivia, who nodded, "yes."

As they got up to leave, Stella realized she was more than a little tipsy. "That sake's really strong. I've never had it before, but it certainly hits the spot," she smiled happily, all cares rapidly disappearing.

Olivia grabbed her arm and they walked outside. "We need that stroll on the Boardwalk now."

Twilight had descended; soon it would be dark. The dog walkers were out and joined by neighbors heading for their local Boardwalk bars and an evening of drinking and companionship and relaxation with friends and visitors alike. Boardwalk vendors had packed up and left. Most businesses were closed or closing up, except one, which Olivia pulled Stella towards.

"Let's get tattoos!"

Stella balked. "We're drunk."

"Perfect! That'll make it less painful! I've always wanted to get a tattoo, haven't you?"

Stella admitted she had as they stepped over the threshold of the little storefront.

"Welcome to *Get Inked*." A woman about their own age with pink hair sat drawing by the counter.

Stella's eye roamed over dozens of sheets of flash containing hundreds of tattoo choices which lined the walls as Olivia asked the woman how much and how long would it take.

"An hour-and-a-half, maybe two depending on what you want," pink hair replied naming price ranges.

"I'm leaning towards a Goth warrior queen." Olivia told her. "Maybe you should get one of those, too." She turned towards Stella whose eye had fallen on a sheet of Chinese characters by the door.

"Those are Kanji tattoos," pink hair said. "Words like 'Peace' or 'Harmony.'"

"I need 'Love,'" Stella said wistfully.

"Ditto that," Olivia and pink hair muttered in unison.

"Wait a minute, you're not drunk, are you?" Pink hair was close enough to get a whiff of their breath as Stella and Olivia signed releases stating they were over the age of eighteen and knew exactly what they were doing.

"Just a teeny bit," Stella reassured her, as Olivia said "Not really," at the same time.

"People faint from heat exhaustion if they've been drinking on a hot afternoon," the woman told them.

"We're lucky it's evening and not summertime then," Stella smiled, now fully on board with Olivia's idea of getting inked.

The woman nodded and called towards the back of the store. "Hans!"

A muscular blonde man in a sleeveless tee shirt, cargo shorts and flip-flops came out from behind a curtain, a needle cartridge filled with dye in hand.

"I can do one of you and he can do the other," the woman said, indicating two reclining chairs as she filled another needle cartridge with dye.

"He can do mine." Olivia smiled broadly at Hans and headed for the nearest recliner.

CHAPTER 23

An hour-and-a-half later, Stella and Olivia staggered out onto the Boardwalk as Hans and the shop owner waved goodbye and shut up business for the night.

"My arm hurts," Olivia whined.

"You're a Goth Warrior Queen; think of it as just a little pinprick." Stella checked her own upper arm. "'Love' hurts, too."

"I don't think I can drive home."

Olivia *was* a little unsteady on her feet, Stella thought. But then, so was she. *Sake is powerful.*

"You can stay at my place. I have an extra Murphy bed."

They stood on the Boardwalk looking left towards *Billy's*, and right towards the Santa Monica Pier lit up with lights twinkling against the night sky.

"I'm not ready to go to bed yet. It's too early." Suddenly, Olivia had decided she didn't hurt so much.

"We need to walk off the sake a bit more," Stella agreed.

Fifteen minutes later they were leaning over the pier railings amongst a smattering of night fishermen watching dark waves roll in from the horizon towards the beach.

"This is more like it." Stella sighed with satisfaction

"More like what?"

"A holiday. A break from all the problems of the past few weeks. I'm really glad you came down to visit, Olivia. I'm enjoying this evening."

"Does anyone resent you turning up and staying in your late aunt's apartment?" Olivia wondered.

Stella thought about this. "You mean like one of Aunt Barb's tenants?

"Yeah."

"Not overtly. I think they're more worried about a rent increase or having to find somewhere else to live if the building's sold."

Olivia nodded. "Understandable. The money interests from other places are moving in with a vengeance and flipping property as fast as they can for a quick profit. I read in the newspaper that long-time LA residents are having to move out and head for more affordable climes."

"Money makes some people do desperate things," Stella agreed, "whether you have it, or not."

"I'm getting hypnotized watching the waves gliding by," Olivia surmised. "It's like there's a heaving, swelling monster out there in the dark."

Stella laughed as they both turned and leaned their backs against the railing. She recalled her dream of the Night Mother. "I think of it more like the earth's being rocked in a giant cradle."

The two women were quiet for a moment, watching people stroll along the pier under strands of colored twinkling lights.

"We're both still drunk." Stella lifted her eyes to the balmy evening breeze. "Fancy a ride on the Ferris wheel?"

"If we're still drunk, we might throw up all that delicious food we ate."

"Nah." Stella grabbed Olivia's elbow. "You're a Goth Warrior Queen, remember?"

Olivia let herself be dragged towards the big wheel much like she'd dragged Stella into the tattoo parlor.

The night air embraced them as they slowly rose over the dark sea far below, and Olivia pointed out places of interest as the living map of Los Angeles unfolded before them.

"That's Malibu to the north where the hills look like a diamond necklace as the lighted roads loop up from Pacific Coast Highway into the Santa Monica Mountains."

Stella followed Olivia's finger along the ridge-line inland towards the Los Angeles Basin and the grid of lights stretching far and wide.

"The giant pulsing heartbeat of the city stretches over the dry bed of a prehistoric sea; deep rivers run below in cavernous faults and fissures," Olivia informed her. "You've got the Hollywood Hills on our distant left and further along there somewhere is my little house in Echo Park. Straight ahead of us in the far, far distance you can just make out the San Gabriel Mountains. To their right and coming back this way towards us, that little clump of shadows is Baldwin Hills." She swung her finger all the way down the coastline. "And there we have Manhattan Beach, Redondo Beach and places south right down to the Palos Verdes Peninsula."

"It's big, so spread out. No wonder it takes a while to drive anywhere," Stella said.

"Let's not get started on the traffic," Olivia said, as the last people took their seats below them and the Ferris wheel rose higher and faster, then plunged downwards.

"What a rush!" Olivia shouted. "I haven't done this since I was a kid at the county fair! Only this time it's like we're plunging down into the waves."

"Arrgghh," they both screamed before rising up again.

"I feel as if I'm flying," Stella said breathlessly, her short black hair whipped back from her face like little wings in the soft evening breeze.

Round and around they went. Neither of them threw up, but when it stopped, both felt a little dizzy. Stella gripped Olivia's arm when they finally staggered off onto solid ground.

"I can see waves breaking against the pylons below us through the cracks in the wooden planks," Olivia said.

"Eyes up, eyes up. Don't look down." Stella jerked Olivia upright. "Whoa!" The pier shuddered as a large wave passed beneath them. "Okay, back to *Billy's* toute de suite."

"Can't we take a taxi?" Olivia pleaded.

"It's not far. Couple miles, tops. A brisk walk will do us good." Stella held Olivia's arm firmly as they descended the steps to the Boardwalk.

"Damn Europeans. You walk everywhere," Olivia grumbled.

It was after midnight when they reached the white picket fence and walked through to the garden separating the two apartment buildings.

"I can't see anything. It's pitch black in here and all fuzzy now that the fog's rolled in," Olivia complained as she hung onto Stella.

"Don't worry. I know the way," Stella reassured her.

It was the last thing she said before something hit her on the head and they both fell to the ground.

CHAPTER 24

I'm never drinking sake again. Stella's head was pounding. Where in the hell was she? It smelled like a sewer. She could see outlines and shades of darkness as her eyes adjusted to the lack of light, but something was stuck over her mouth; she couldn't open it, or move her hands, which were tied behind her. Her feet were also bound. She was lying on her side in something that felt like damp sand. Olivia lay next to her on her stomach, head turned towards Stella, eyes closed. Was she dead? Stella wiggled her body an inch closer and bent her head down. No. Olivia was snoring softly. She'd been dribbling in her sleep, too. The duct tape at the corner of her mouth had become unstuck. Stella gave her a sharp poke with her elbow. Olivia's eyes flew open. Stella could see the whites as the tip of Olivia's tongue loosened the corner of the duct tape more.

"Ot hapnd?"

Stella could only moan and shake her head slightly, but she became aware of another smell, a feral smell. They were beside some sort of post. She tried to use it as leverage and sit up, but only bumped her head. They were underneath some wooden floorboards. While Olivia stretched her jaws and worked her tongue at the duct tape, Stella wriggled around trying to see something. Anything. A very faint light was coming in from the outside through some broken mesh vents. At the far end she could make out shapes of bikes and surfboards.

"Where the hell are we?" Olivia had worked enough tape loose to speak more coherently.

Something slithered by them. Stella's eyes widened in fear. *Cripes!* The Snake and Parrot Man's missing python! And it was much bigger than she remembered! Stella sincerely hoped the reptile wasn't hungry as she swore she could see its tongue flickering out between its jaws and its beady little eyes glittering in the darkness.

"Aaaarrgghh." Stella's mouth snapped open so abruptly into a wide "O," that she ripped the tape loose along with any hair she had on her upper lip. "Owwch!" Her eyes teared up in sudden pain.

The snake backed off.

"Omigod! Are we in hell?" Olivia panicked.

"We're in the basement at *Billy's.*" Tears ran down Stella's cheeks. "Someone's stashed us up on the sand and dirt foundation end."

"Who would do such a thing?" Olivia cried. "And why?"

"I don't know. But I think we need to get out of here, quick."

Stella was frightened, but her anger was building. Anger at their unseen assailant as she realized there was an enemy out there; an enemy who'd tried to run her over in the supermarket parking lot. An enemy who probably pushed Auntie Barb down the stairs on the night she'd arrived in Venice. And this enemy had probably killed poor, lustful Andrea, too.

"I may have 'Love' tattooed on my upper arm, but I've got a Goth Warrior Queen by my side, and in my heart of hearts,

I'm one, too. Goddammit!" Stella raised her bound feet as high as she could and kicked an old suitcase out of the way. "Come on, Olivia. Before whoever it is comes back." She started wriggling and writhing towards the bike and surfboard shapes and the basement door she knew was beyond them, kicking aside more old suitcases and storage boxes in the way. "Or, before we get eaten."

"I don't think she's hungry. That snake's got a budge in its middle." Olivia was wriggling along right behind her. "I think she's already eaten."

Stella paused. *Of course. Hitler! Greg's missing cat!* "How do you know it's a she?"

"She's got a little nest over there."

Stella turned her head and in the dim light could just make out the python coiling up on a clutch of eggs.

"She's gonna be a mommy!" Distressed and terrorized as she was, Olivia was practically cooing.

"She's not an art project; she's a Boardwalk entertainer." Stella refused to allow any image of baby snakes slithering around the apartments to cross her mind. The sound of a vehicle approaching and stopping beside the building made her heart beat faster. "Come on Olivia, focus. We have to get out of here!"

They'd almost reached the edge of where the sand and dirt foundation dropped down four feet to where the concrete floor began when they heard footsteps on the basement steps. The doorknob rattled; then the door creaked wide open.

Shit!

A man stood silhouetted in the doorway. Stella couldn't see his face, but he wore a hat reminiscent of a 1940's gangster.

CHAPTER 25

Stella's eyes followed his arm reaching up and out. She hoped the hand at the end of it wasn't holding a gun, but the basement then flooded with a dim flickering light; he'd pulled the string dangling down from the light bulb fixture. Both she and Olivia held their breath as he recoiled in shock at the sight of the women.

"Who are you?"

"Who the hell are you?" Stella countered.

"I'm Bill Craven."

So this was the man who'd sold Aunt Barb the apartment building! Stella ramped up her inner warrior queen. "I'm Stella, Stella Maris."

"Barb's English niece." Craven smiled, before pulling out a Swiss army knife from his jacket pocket and flicking it open as he walked towards them. Someone else was padding down the steps behind him.

Olivia let out a frightened squeak. Stella ramped up her inner warrior queen another notch. Yes, she was English. She was not going down without a fight. Stiff upper lip, her mother would have said, quoting her own mother's mantra. She got ready for another kick.

My head aches but my abdominals are really getting a workout tonight with the leg lifts.

He stood over them, knife in hand. "What are you two doing down here? And why have you got zip ties around your hands and feet?"

"Er." Stella was confused. Now he was slicing through her ties.

Clearly, this man had not expected to encounter anyone in the basement in the middle of the night. More importantly, he didn't seem to be a murderous monster with a threatening disposition. He was an old man in his late sixties, with a dog that had padded down the basement steps and stood alongside its master wagging its tail in a friendly way.

"This is Jupiter." The canine licked Stella's bare toes as Bill cut Olivia loose.

"We've been trying to reach you," Stella told him as she and Olivia scrambled down from the bank of sand and dirt, rubbing their wrists and ankles.

"And I've been trying to reach Barbara,"

I should get an answering machine even though I'm not staying long.

"I wanted to tell her I was on my way. Have a few things to take care of here. But right this minute I need a cup of coffee. Me and Jupiter just drove in from Idaho. It's still a few hours until dawn, but I didn't want to disturb Barbara in the middle of the night. Thought I'd just collect this." He reached back and grabbed one of the old suitcases. "Forgot it when I left. What the hell?" He'd spied the python in the far corner.

Jupiter had spied it, too. Bill grabbed the dog's collar with his free hand.

"She's an escaped Boardwalk entertainer," Stella told him. "The Snake and Parrot Man will be out front in the morning and I'll let him know where to find her."

"I knew I'd run into craziness while I was here; I just didn't expect it so soon," Bill mumbled.

"Let's get out of this place," Olivia pleaded. "My head hurts and whoever knocked us out might come back."

"I've been trying to reach your aunt for several weeks."

Bill Craven, Stella and Olivia were sitting at the dining-room table with fresh cups of black coffee. Stella and Olivia were applying cold washcloths to the back of their heads; both had slight bumps, but luckily the skin was not broken. Bill had removed his hat and carefully placed it on top of the suitcase beside him. Mr. Velvet sat in the ratty old armchair glaring at Jupiter, who kept a respectful distance.

"I wanted to ask Barbara to dig out the suitcase and send it to me via UPS. Then circumstances changed, and since I hadn't been able to reach her, I drove out here stopping to call periodically along the way."

He looked sad. Stella had told him Aunt Barb was dead.

"Wish I hadn't gone to see an old pal of mine in Oregon now for those few days." He sighed. "Shouldn't have made that little side trip to the Napa Valley, either, but I was so close and wanted to bring Barbara a bottle of wine she likes from there." He looked up from his coffee with a small smile. "They don't sell it in stores. You can only get it at the winery."

All three were quiet for a moment sipping their coffee. Jupiter got up to have a drink of water from the bowl Stella had put down for him in the kitchen. Mr. Velvet's eyes monitored the dog's movements.

"Stella, d'you have any Tylenol? My head's still pounding from whoever knocked us out." Olivia shielded her eyes from the overhead light. Stella had turned the dimmer switch way down. They were sitting in a kind of twilight, but it was obviously still too bright for the artist.

"Let me take a look."

Stella got up and went into the bathroom to rummage through the cabinet above the wash basin. After selecting a small bottle labeled *Aspirin 325 mg.*, she detected movement from the corner of her eye outside the bathroom window. Was that the person who'd knocked them out and stashed them in the basement? Quietly, she unlocked the bathroom door and peeked out. Nothing. Heart pounding, Stella slipped out onto the back porch. Nothing. And nothing moved in the garden below.

Relax. You've just had a knock on the head. Plus, you're hungover from the saki.

Stella shut the bathroom door and locked it, then checked the window to make sure the latch was fastened before going back to the dining room.

"Will this do?" She handed the bottle of aspirin to Olivia after selecting four for herself.

"It'll have to."

Bill Craven watched the women chug down the pain relievers with gulps of coffee. "Are you sure you don't want me to drive you to the hospital to get checked out?"

"I don't have health insurance," Stella told him.

"Me either," Olivia added.

"Shouldn't you at least file a police report?" Bill looked concerned.

Stella pictured herself facing Sergeant Martinez. "I don't feel up to it right this minute."

Olivia agreed. "I'd rather wait for daylight when my head feels a bit clearer. Hopefully."

Stella studied Bill as he drank his coffee. "You really drove all the way back from Idaho just to pick up a suitcase?" She wondered what was in it.

"No. I got a call from Gary Edwards. He said both my aunt and her friend had deteriorating health. He was concerned, thought I might want to come and have a look first hand, see if they needed to go into assisted living."

"Who's your aunt?" Stella tried to recall any old ladies she'd seen or heard about since she'd arrived.

Bill nodded towards Speedway. "Vi. She's 96. Lives with her lifelong companion, Edna, in the green-gabled house over there."

"The old ladies fighting over the trash cans?"

Bill chuckled. "That sounds like them. They've been arguing with each other ever since I remember."

"I thought they were sisters."

"That's what everyone was led to believe. I thought that myself when I was little. Things were different years ago. They wanted to stay safe. And the years went by and everyone just assumed."

How sad. But in the old days people didn't talk about themselves like they do nowadays. And everyone has secrets they don't want others to know.

Stella wondered if their violence extended beyond themselves. Her neighbor, Carol, had mentioned they didn't like younger women. Surely, at such an advanced age they couldn't have *that* much energy to knock out Olivia and herself, tie both of their hands and feet, then stash them in the basement. And why would they? She dismissed the thought.

"One of them hit the other with their walking stick. Carol and I both saw it."

"Who's Carol?" Olivia picked up the coffee pot. "Refill?"

"Next door," Stella told her, as she and Bill both pushed their mugs forward.

Bill sighed. "I tried to get them to sell the house and move into a rest home before I left for Idaho, but they wouldn't have it. They always were independent, not to mention stubborn, and both seemed to be in good health mentally and physically. For their age, I mean. Gary and his mom said they'd keep an eye on them for me." He sighed again. "That's why I had to come back. Not only for the suitcase." He took a long swallow of coffee."

"Stella was curious. "Did you grow up in that house."

Bill nodded. "I did. Along with my Mom, Vi's sister."

"And you just moved across the street to," she looked around the apartment, "this place?"

"No. I was in the Navy and gone for years. But before that, my dad owned these apartments. He died when I was a kid and left the property to me. Mom painted *Billy's* on the front door. She took care of things until I grew up and for years while I was away."

"Then you came back..." Olivia prompted.

"After the Navy, I came back and stayed, but I never lived here. And then one day I met your Aunt Barbara. She and her musician husband were given notice to vacate their rental cottage on one of the canals as it had been sold to a developer. This apartment had just become vacant so they moved in. He died shortly after. She eventually bought the place. And here we are."

"I need to talk to you some more," Stella looked at Olivia whose head was drooping. "But it's been a long night and I think we're both very tired."

Olivia nodded in agreement.

"Me, too. It's been a long drive." Bill Craven looked at his watch. "It's four thirty a.m. Hour of the wolf."

Stella and Olivia looked at him blankly. He smiled.

"The hour before dawn according to the great Ingmar Bergman." He reached for his hat and stood up. "Swedish film director from the sixties. Goodnight, ladies. Come on, Jupiter."

Bill glanced out of the window towards Speedway. "Ah, the light just went on over at Green Gables. The aunties are awake. He placed his hat firmly on his head and picked up the old suitcase. "Pray for me."

"I'm sure they'll be delighted to see you," Olivia said.

Stella wasn't so sure as she walked the sprightly old man and his dog to the front door. Those two would be a nightmare for other tenants in assisted living. After they finished screaming at their nephew. She was still curious about what was in the suitcase but English reserve kept her from prying. Olivia, however had no hesitation.

"What've you got in that old case, anyway?"

Bill turned to the women and smiled. "Love letters."

"Wow." Olivia said dreamily.

Stella recovered from this admission first, and opened the door. "Thank you for rescuing us. I don't know what would have happened if you hadn't come along when you did."

"Anything for Barbara's niece. I was fond of that gal." He looked sad again. "We'll talk again real soon. Make sure all your doors are firmly locked," Bill advised as he descended the stairs.

"Whatta guy," Olivia remarked. "So romantic! And lovely blue eyes and silver hair!"

She and Stella watched from the window as he walked across Speedway under the corner streetlight, opened the back gate of the green-gabled house, and disappeared into the shadows of its garden.

CHAPTER 26

Stella opened her eyes to bright sunshine streaming through the open window blinds that she hadn't bothered to close last night. She hadn't bothered to undress, either, just fallen fully clothed onto the bed after she pulled it down from the wall. Olivia lay snoring on the Murphy bed in the dining-room. She hadn't bothered to take off her clothes or get under the duvet, either. Mr. Velvet was curled up by her feet. *Traitor. Maybe he'd like to go and live with Olivia and her dogs after I go back to England.*

Stella yawned and thought about last night. Who had done this to her and Olivia? And why? Bill Craven had rescued them in the nick of time before the perpetrator had returned to do....what? Kill them and dump their bodies somewhere else? She shivered, then felt her anger blossom. Screw whoever it was. How dare they try and frighten two bold and beautiful women! She would not cave in to fear, and she had a feeling Olivia wouldn't either. Stella looked at her watch. Almost noon. She should file a police report. Sergeant Martinez unnerved her with his flirty, intimidating way, but she could cope with almost anything if she had enough sleep. And a cup of tea. Or two. Time to get going.

She sat up. Her wrists and ankles still felt a little sore from the zip ties, but her headache was down to a dull ache and the slight swelling had gone down completely. Stella got out of bed and stretched, yawning again.

"You were talking in your sleep." Olivia was awake. "Mumbling about some little black book. Ouch!" She felt the back of her head gingerly as she sat up. "Screw that bastard who thought he'd get the better of us!"

"My sentiments exactly."

Stella explained her dreams by the Night Mother and the Great Mother, pointing to her aunt's bookshelves as they drank a pot of fresh coffee and downed more aspirin, Olivia had nixed the idea of tea saying her head still ached from a mixture of being hit plus a hangover, she couldn't differentiate, but coffee would help a lot.

"Aunt Barb used black sketchbooks as her journals."

"And so many of them," How can you tell which one the Mothers meant?"

"Exactly."

"Only one way to find out." Olivia started pulling some diaries off the shelves, patting the little stack beside her. "How about we take half each?'

"But you don't know what you're looking for."

"Neither do you."

"True," Stella admitted. She indicated the front room. "There's more on the shelf in there."

"Oh, goody. I love a project." Fueled by coffee and painkillers, Olivia was energized by the thought of reading hundreds of pages of someone else's life. "But first I have to call my neighbor and ask him to feed the dogs for me."

"He won't mind?"

"No. He often does that, takes them for walks in the park, too, if I'm busy." Olivia reached for the phone.

"We should report the attack, too."

Stella shook some Kitty Kibbles into Mr. Velvet's bowl, then took her coffee into the other room, pushed her bed into the wall with one hand and latched it. She finished the coffee while selecting some clean clothes and putting them on. When she walked back into the dining-room Olivia was in the bathroom. Stella could hear water splashing in the wash basin.

"Refreshed and ready to go." Olivia opened the bathroom door and came out.

"Do you need to borrow something to wear?

"No. I always carry a spare pair of panties in my purse. Just in case plans change, like they did last night."

"Sounds sensible."

Together they pushed the spare Murphy bed back into the wall and latched it. "Good use of space." Olivia looked around the small apartment.

"The coffee and aspirin are doing their job, but I need to eat something to combat the acid in my stomach now."

Stella pulled a box of water crackers out of the pantry for them to munch on.

"These'll tide us over. I need to let the Snake and Parrot man know where his reptile is."

They found him in his usual spot on the Boardwalk, one arm covered in parrots. The rest of the macaws perched on the baby buggy handle. An iguana sat inside wearing a little sweater against the chill from a stiff breeze blowing off the ocean. Snake and Parrot Man, "call me Bob," was ecstatic when he heard the news about his python. Just then Sergeant Martinez and his partner slowly rolled by in their patrol car.

Bob held up his free arm. "Stop! They found my Monty!" he told them through the open window as he pointed at Stella. "He's in her basement."

"You may have to rename him." Stella ignored the amused look that appeared on Martinez's face. *"She's* hatching eggs down there."

"Yah, you might have to call your snake Minerva," Olivia suggested.

"Minnie?" Bob tried the name on for size. "Miss Minnie? I like it."

"How about *Mrs.* Minnie," Olivia corrected.

The police officers looked at each other, parked their vehicle and climbed out, ready to investigate.

"Okay, let's get this over with."

Did Sergeant Martinez actually roll his eyes? Stella felt defensive.

"You stay out here." Snake and Parrot man said to his girlfriend as he off-loaded the birds from his arm to her.

Stella led the way through the garden to the basement,

"This is the third time we've been to this address in what– about two weeks?" Martinez noted, "Plus the incident by the Marina jetty. Do dead bodies accompany you wherever you go Ms. Maris? Human – or otherwise?" he added dryly. His partner chuckled.

"Nothing that's happened in this, this" she bit back the word 'godforsaken' "place is my doing!" Stella snapped back, opening the basement door. She pulled the dangling cord from the ceiling. The bare light bulb flickered on, then off, then on again.

"There." She pointed to where the reptile lay curled up on her eggs.

Both cops stopped looking amused.

"I'm not going near that." Sergeant Martinez's partner involuntarily took a step back.

"Me either," Martinez placed his hand on his gun. "We need to call Animal Control."

"How about the zoo?"

"No-o-o." Snake and Parrot Man crawled up onto the sand and dirt foundation. "Come to Daddy, baby," he cooed.

The python's tongue flickered.

"She looks smaller in daylight," Olivia observed.

Martinez looked at the women. "Oh?"

"We were assaulted last night," Stella explained. "Someone hit us both on the head and bundled us up under here."

"We need to make a police report," Olivia added.

Martinez held both his hands up. "Whoa. First things first. Let's deal with the item on hand. Then you can tell us," he hesitated for a fraction of a second, "the other story." His partner, Officer Baker, had stepped back by the door and was talking into his shoulder phone.

"You're so beautiful, Little Mama," Bob baby-talked to his pet, who was starting to uncoil.

The snake opened her mouth and showed her fangs. Martinez put his hand back on his gun ready to draw.

"You're making her nervous," Bob cried.

She's not the only one that's nervous, Stella noted as everyone tensed up. Monty aka Minnie started slowly slithering towards them. Martinez drew his gun, but held it down by his side.

"You shoot my snake and I'll sue your ass!" Bob shouted.

"Threaten me, and I'll arrest your ass," Martinez countered.

Stella glanced to her left and picked up a large suitcase, quickly turning it upside down and emptying it. Moldy old clothes tumbled onto the basement floor. "Here," she threw the empty suitcase over to the Snake and Parrot Man. "Put her in there."

Bob caught it, bundled his beloved pet inside, and snapped the latches shut. "What about her eggs?"

Stella picked up an old Easter basket that had seen better days and threw that over to him. "This should be large enough."

"Well done, Ms. Maris," Sergeant Martinez looked at her admiringly. "Cancel Animal Control," he told his partner.

Bob climbed down from the sand and dirt. "You can carry the eggs," he said to Officer Baker, glaring at Martinez as he walked out the basement door clutching the old suitcase with its precious contents. "I'm going home."

"I volunteer to fill out the Incident Report on this one," Baker said to Martinez, as both officers chuckled and followed him out.

"I'll be up to interview you two in a minute," Martinez told the women as Stella shut the basement door behind them all. "Don't go anywhere."

"I need tortillas," Olivia whispered to her friend. "They're my go-to comfort food in times of stress. I'll get some breakfast things from the mini-market and be right back."

"Okay." Stella hadn't a clue what tortillas were, but if Olivia needed them, she needed them.

Everyone trooped out to the Boardwalk except Stella, who turned to go back up to the apartment.

"Psstt." Sam was peeking out of his back door. "Have the cops gone?"

"For a minute or two. They're coming back. Were you at home last night, Sam?"

He shook his head. "No. I've been staying at a friend's place since the cops released me after the questioning about–you know." He looked sad. "I just came back for some clean clothes. I feel awful about what happened to Andrea." His eyes teared up. "I just can't be in my apartment right now. I don't want to move, but I may have to. Memories, you know."

"Have you heard anything more about what happened to her?" Stella couldn't bring herself to say the word "murder." It sounded so gruesome and Sam seemed genuinely heartbroken.

He shook his head. "Nothing."

"What time did you get here?" Stella was curious. The basement was under his apartment. If he'd come back for clean clothes in the middle of the night he might have heard something. There was only a layer of wooden floorboards in his apartment with various water and heating pipes running underneath, no insulation from what she could see. And both of the women hadn't been exactly quiet. Neither had Bill Craven.

"I got here about ten minutes ago," Sam replied. "I heard voices down in the cellar. Why are the police here again?"

Stella told him the Snake and Parrot man's python had been found.

"That's one piece of good news, I guess."

Men's voices coming in from the Boardwalk floated down between the buildings.

"Sorry, but I have to quick grab a few things and get out of here. I'll be back in a few days and let you know what I decide to do." Sam quickly shut the door as the officers walked down the garden path.

Martinez and Baker sat at the dining table with Stella while Olivia busied herself at the kitchen stove heating up a can of beans and scrambling eggs

"Excuse me doing this, but we're starving. Last night was very traumatic." She threw a tortilla on the gas ring to heat up.

"No problem." Officer Martinez opened his little note book. "Okay, let's review. You come for a vacation with your aunt."

He looked up at Stella, who nodded. "Vacation" sounded so much saner than "emotionally furious spur-of-the-minute escape" to her ears. And everyone else's she hoped. Especially the police.

"You arrive here around midnight and find your aunt–who you've never met before–dead at the bottom of the stairs."

Stella nodded again. Thank God her headache had eased up.

"It's ruled an accident. Then, while you're out on bike ride in the middle of arranging her funeral, you find a dead body washed up on the Marina jetty."

"Er, no. Some children playing on the beach did. I just happened to be present. Along with several others," she added.

"Right," Martinez consulted his notes again. "That guy turned out to be a Brit, too."

Stella felt Officer Baker's eyes bore into her. She sensed Olivia's ears prick up at this bit of news. She'd stopped scrambling the eggs.

"What can I say. England is an island," Stella pointed out. "It gets crowded. We've traveled everywhere for hundreds of years. Venice Beach is a vacation spot," she shrugged. "As well as a neighborhood."

Martinez looked skeptical. "Did you know him? The dead man?"

"No," Stella answered truthfully. She wasn't about to confess that she knew his brother. Vaguely. That he was her ex-boyfriend's new lover. Or that she'd impetuously fled England on a whim the same day Brian had told her he was leaving her for Nigel. It was just a coincidence Nigel had seen Stella on the Boardwalk when he'd turned up to identify and claim his brother's body, wasn't it? She also pushed the part about them having an argument over Brian to the back of her mind. It sounded bad. And it wasn't relevant. Was it?

"You look confused Ms. Maris." Now it was the sergeant's eyes boring into her.

"I am," she admitted. "And very upset," she added staunchly and loudly.

"All right, all right." Martinez held his hand up. "Calm down. let's continue. Next thing is one of your aunt's tenants, Andrea, is found dead on the beach right in front of these apartments."

"I don't know what to tell you. I barely spoke to her," Stella said helplessly, at the same time recalling Andrea's flirtatiousness. She'd seen her canoodling with Sam at her aunt's funeral, and over dinner at a café with another man. There was also the bird-call guy on a bicycle, not to mention a husband somewhere that Carol had told her about. Surely, the police had already found out about Andrea's love life during the investigation? She didn't feel the need to reiterate.

"How is that investigation going by the way," Stella asked. "Any news?"

Now it was Sergeant Martinez's turn to shrug. "What can I say, it's ongoing. Now tell us about last night."

"Someone tried to kill us." Olivia had turned off the stove, put a lid on the beans, covered the eggs and wrapped the tortillas in foil to keep them warm. She came and joined them at the table, sitting on the remaining chair.

Stella blinked. Again, why? She still didn't understand how all the events were connected.

"Details, step by step," Martinez ordered, looking seriously from one woman to the other. "And I need your name and relationship to Ms. Maris here."

"I'm Stella's friend, Olivia Rodriguez." She gave him her address in Echo Park.

"Thank you."

"We went to dinner," Stella told him.

"At what time?" Baker asked.

"Early. Five-ish," Stella replied.

"Then we went for tattoos." Olivia showed them her Goth Warrior Queen.

"Very nice," Martinez observed.

Both officers looked expectantly at Stella, who reluctantly pulled up her sleeve, exposing the Kanji tattoo.

"She got 'Love,'" Olivia explained.

Martinez smiled. "Charming."

"It was dark by then, but still early, so we walked to the pier," Stella said, feeling no need to explain that they were both still drunk from dinner and wishing Martinez would quit with that little smile of his.

"Where did you eat?" he asked.

They told him. Both officers nodded.

"Great place," Baker commented. "And where did you get your tattoos?"

Olivia and Stella looked at each other. Neither of them could remember.

"On the Boardwalk somewhere. Not far from the restaurant," Stella said.

"Okay." Martinez jotted something down in his notebook. "So you walked to the pier, then what?"

"We took a ride on the Ferris wheel," Olivia told them.

"Sounds like fun," Baker said.

"It was fabulous," Olivia blurted out.

"Yes, it was," Stella agreed.

"And very vacation-ey," Martinez surmised. "Did you stay long on the pier?"

"Not really. It was getting late, so we walked back."

"Along the Boardwalk," Olivia clarified. "You wouldn't get a taxi, remember?" She looked at Stella.

"The night air was very refreshing." Damn Olivia for implying she was cheap.

"The Boardwalk's not exactly a safe place for two women late at night," Martinez remarked. "I wouldn't advise that in future."

"Got that right," Olivia muttered.

"Because it was late, I suggested Olivia stay the night," Stella said. "We were walking through the garden, and that's the last thing I remember before we woke up in the basement sometime later. I don't know at what time."

She went on to describe what happened next, realizing that someone intended them harm, and trying to escape before that person turned up again.

"Do you have any idea who that person might be?" Officer Martinez looked very serious now.

Stella shook her head. "No. As you know, I haven't been here very long. I barely know anyone." Talking about things, she began to feel scared. Was it a malicious neighbor, or a random perpetrator from the thousands of people traversing the Boardwalk? Maybe she should leave and go back to the UK sooner rather than later. She could stay at her mother's. Mr. Bernstein could take care of things here. She no longer cared about the damn wills.

"How did you free yourselves?" Officer Baker jotted down a few notes now.

"Bill Craven turned up." Stella explained what she knew about her aunt buying the apartment building from him. "He's in town to make new living arrangements for his elderly aunt and her friend. And he came to the basement to collect an old suitcase he'd left there."

"Do you know where we can find him?" Martinez tapped his note book with his pen.

"Right over there." Stella pointed out the window, through the pine tree's branches and towards the green-gabled house on the corner of Speedway.

"Oh, Vi and Edna's," Baker said, as both officers looked in that direction. "Interesting old ladies," he added, chuckling.

"That," Stella couldn't help herself, "has to be the remark of the century."

Martinez smiled, then his attention was caught by something. "There's a cat in that tree."

Sure enough, Mr. Velvet was sitting on a branch staring at them.

"My aunt's cat. The window's his cat door." Stella sincerely hoped the little feline wouldn't make any sudden moves and lunch himself towards them. She remembered Martinez had been quick to put his hand on his sidearm when he'd spied the python. You just couldn't trust guns and split-second responses to sudden moves in her opinion. *My imagination's running wild. I must be really stressed out.*

"Anything else happen that you consider suspicious?" Martinez looked at her, serious again.

"Someone tried to run me down in the supermarket parking lot," Stella blurted out. "And I think somebody was in the apartment when I was out." She explained about the front door being ajar when she returned. "And there's a problem with my aunt's will. Her attorney's busy sorting that out. Plus, there was food poisoning after the funeral and party. No one's complained to me and not everyone got really sick; they seem to have put it down to a hangover. I spent the night on the bathroom floor." Stella's mind was busy knitting events together as she rushed on. "And now," Stella looked at all three people staring at her. "I seriously wonder if Aunt Barb's "accident" was really an accident. Did she fall or was she pushed?"

There. She'd said it. Everything was out in the open. Well, almost everything. She'd left out Nigel and his dead brother. And the bit about Ron's estranged son turning up. A tear had slid down her cheek at the thought of her aunt.

Martinez's concern turned to sympathy. "I'm really sorry," he told Stella, and she believed him. Maybe he wasn't so bad after all.

"And you have absolutely no idea if any one person is responsible for all of these things?" He was very serious again.

Stella shook her head. "No."

The two officers looked meaningfully at each other.

"Do *you* have any idea?" Olivia had caught the look between them.

"We don't," the sergeant admitted, "and we can't comment on any ongoing investigation, you understand, but, rest assured, there is an ongoing investigation, and now," Martinez tapped his notebook, "we'll be adding to it."

He looked at Stella. "Are you sure there's nothing more?"

After a moment's hesitation, she caved in and told them about Nigel. "He's my ex-boyfriend's lover and he was here to identify his dead brother's body, the one that washed up on the rocks."

Both cops perked up.

"Last name?" Martinez practically barked it out as Baker got busy with his notes.

"I don't know, I never met him before." Three pairs of eyes looked at her incredulously. "I mean I know *of* him, I've seen him before, but I've never actually met him before a few days ago. We've never been introduced."

"Where'd you see him?" Baker was genuinely curious.

"In the pub."

The two officers tried to not burst out laughing.

Stella sensed Sergeant Martinez was trying to be patient with her. "Oh-kay." He clasped his hands together and leaned forward, placing his elbows on the table. "A pub in England?"

"Right. We don't know each other, but we know about each other. The only reason he's in Los Angeles was to retrieve his brother's remains. He didn't know I was here. It was a surprise to us both when he recognized me on the Boardwalk. I haven't seen him since," she finished up. *I'm definitely not mentioning the phone call between him and Brian.*

"We can check him out and get his surname from *that* incident report." Sergeant Martinez studied Stella intently, but she beat him to it before he could ask another question.

"And a Canadian claiming to be my aunt's late husband's estranged son stopped by unexpectedly looking for her."

Baker jotted down few more words in his notebook. "And his name was...?" He looked up expectantly.

"Scott. I didn't get his surname, but it may have been the same as Ray's–Smith. I think he's from Toronto, but he didn't give me his address. He didn't stay long."

"Did he say where he was staying?"

"No, but I first saw him playing on the beach with his two little boys near the Santa Monica pier, so it might be round there somewhere."

Martinez and Baker each asked more questions, then finally snapped their notebooks shut and stood up to leave.

The sergeant brought out his business card and scribbled another phone number on it.

"I already have your cards." Stella indicated two cards sitting next to the phone.

"That's the general LAPD and our precinct phone numbers. This is an extra number where you can reach me directly in case of an emergency." He handed it to her. "Don't hesitate to call immediately if anything else happens or you have a suspicion or remember something no matter how insignificant you think it might be."

Stella opened the front door for the officers.

"In the meantime, be very, very careful," Martinez warned both women as he and Baker walked out. "And," he turned back, his foot already on the first stair, "thanks for finding the snake."

Stella closed the door behind them as they clomped down the stairs, but not before hearing Baker say, "People are always saying the Americans are crazy, but I think the Brits take the cake."

"Yeah, but you gotta admit, she's having the holiday from hell," Martinez replied as they walked out onto Speedway.

CHAPTER 27

Olivia scooped beans into her tortilla and added some salsa before rolling it up and holding it in one hand. "Sergeant Martinez is handsome. And I think he likes you." With her other hand she forked up some scrambled eggs. It was breakfast although Olivia called it brunch.

"I think he suspects me of something." Stella dabbed salsa on her eggs. "This stuff definitely perks them up." Stella wasn't overly fond of beans but thought the tortillas a winner.

Mr. Velvet sat in the armchair, sulking. Olivia had shooed him off the table after he'd jumped in from the tree.

"He's blocking my view of the cops," she'd explained as the two women had closed the front door and watched through the window as Baker and Martinez walked over to the green-gabled house.

"I have a class to teach tonight, so I should get going soon. We don't know each other that well, Stella, but I feel a kinship with you after what we went through last night."

"Same here," Stella agreed. It was true she felt comfortable with Olivia.

"I've never been a beach person, and I've only been to Santa Monica and Venice a couple of times in my life, but last night on the Ferris wheel I got a whole new perspective," Olivia said reflectively. "I've never painted the ocean, and I feel a whole new idea coming on."

"Are you sure it wasn't the bump on the head?"

"There is that," she admitted. "I'm worried about you. Something strange is going on around here. If I didn't have to teach the class, I'd offer to stay tonight. I don't like to think of you on your own. Would you like me to come and stay with you tomorrow for a few days? I could even bring the dogs."

Stella chuckled. "I'm sure Mr. Velvet would be thrilled at that. Truth is, I feel like leaving and going home sooner than later at the moment. But I'm not entirely alone. Carol next door is a good neighbor."

"I understand. But we could go through your aunt's diaries." Olivia nodded towards credenza where they'd stacked the few she'd pulled down from the shelf. "You have to honor the dreams. The Mothers are trying to help you."

Stella nodded.

"And what about hanging the painting while you're here?"

Stella looked at Olivia's gift, propped against the wall. She should enjoy it properly, even if it was only for a short while. "I'd like you to stay–you'd be very welcome–but your dogs would probably be very unhappy if you brought them here."

"Yeah, you're right. They're used to a larger space. I have classes to teach, too. From my house it doesn't take long to drive to my job. From here the freeway commute would be a nightmare."

"Perhaps an over-nighter on the weekend, instead?" Stella suggested. "Then you can arrange for your neighbor to take care of the dogs." Stella liked dogs, but in no way could she imagine those two huge canine bodies in the small apartment.

Olivia nodded, "Sounds good. As long as you're sure you'll be okay until then."

"I will," Stella promised. "I won't go out after dark. And, I have Mr. Velvet to keep me company."

"A guard cat; I like it." Olivia pushed her empty plate away. "But before I leave, let's at least hang the painting."

Wall space was limited, but they found a place by the phone, then stood back to contemplate.

"Looks great there," Stella decided.

Olivia picked up her shoulder bag to leave and then reached over for one of the diaries laying on the credenza. "Pity we don't have time to look at these right now." She flipped a page. "Your aunt's writing is very small."

Stella moved closer so she could see, too. "I think she was trying to cram as much as she could on each page."

"Listen to this, Stella: *'Omigod I'm thirty years old today and I'm still not married.'*" Olivia read out loud. "Your aunt's in crisis!" Olivia's eyes were glued to the page.

Stella sighed. It was the age-old female dilemma. Maybe Barbara hadn't been so unconventional after all, but didn't every human being yearn to be loved? Yearn to love someone and have them love you back? Someone you could share with; someone you could depend on who would stick by your side?

She and Olivia read on silently for a few moments. It seemed that Ray and Barbara had broken up and was difficult to decipher in places, especially where a tear had dropped onto the words and smudged them. The emotions poured out onto the page all those years ago were all too familiar to both women.

"Oh, this is good, Stella. It's like a telenovela!"

"What year was it written?" Stella took the book from Olivia and turned back a few pages. "1977. Tell you what, I'm going to pull all the black books off of the shelves, look at the dates of each one, then set aside the most recent ones, say the last three years for us to read this weekend." She closed the diary and stuck it back on the bookshelf.

"But I want to see how the romance turns out."

Stella smiled. "They reconcile."

"Now you've spoilt it for me."

"Ray and Barbara get married."

"A happy ending then." Olivia sighed and hitched her purse higher up on her shoulder. "Okay, now I don't have to read it."

Stella walked her to the door. "Are you sure you're okay to drive?"

"I'm fine. Just a slight headache now," Olivia replied.

"Well, take care."

"You, too."

"See you Saturday."

CHAPTER 28

After her friend left, Stella washed the dishes, refilled Mr. Velvet's bowl with Kitty Kibbles, took two more aspirin, then spent the rest of the afternoon pulling each diary down from the shelves in both rooms, and checking the date her aunt had written on the front page. Sometimes there wasn't one, or she couldn't decipher it because of coffee stains or illegible writing. Sometimes she couldn't find a date until halfway through book, or the year had been left off. *Pity you weren't as neat with your thoughts as you were with your files Aunt Barb.* But then, who was? Especially where emotions were concerned. She turned to the last diary to check the date and flipped through the pages. There wasn't one; she took it in the other room and put it with the others that she and Olivia would read. Everything else dated before 1990 she put on the shelves in the best date order she could muster as Harry Bernstein had suggested.

It was quite late when she finished. The sun had gone down and night would soon descend. Stella yawned. She was hungry. Rummaging through the freezer, she pulled out a spinach quiche and turned the oven on to heat up. Mr.

Velvet rubbed against her legs. She picked him up and gently scratched his head. He started purring loudly.

"I'm onto you. How come you always turn up when there's food around?" she whispered in his ear.

He purred louder. She noticed his cat bowl was almost empty.

"You better not have a tapeworm."

He stopped purring and wriggled to get down.

"Okay, okay." She reached into the larder and pulled out a can of cat food for him, then put the quiche into the oven, setting the timer for thirty minutes.

While her dinner heated, she had a soak in the claw-foot bathtub relaxing in scented water. Her aunt had an array of aromatic oils. Tonight, Stella had chosen almond oil because it was mixed with aloe gel and other ingredients the label specified would soothe any aches and pains. The phone rang. It was her mother.

"Listen, darling. Quick catch-up and I have to tell you something."

Stella could hear samba music in the background. "How's Jim?"

"On the mend, but not totally up and about yet."

"It must be the middle of the night there."

"It is, but you know how the continentals are. Eating late and dancing until 3 a.m." Sheila's voice sounded a little slurred. "I'm out with a friend."

"When are you going back to England?"

"The doctor thinks Jim can travel next week, so we'll be going home then. When are *you* going back?"

"Pretty soon." Stella briefly explained that now the funeral was over she thought Barbara's lawyer could take care of things.

"Very sensible, darling. Listen, earlier on today, my friend and I–she's English too, but she lives here in Spain–went to see this gypsy fortune teller, who was very positive, very accurate when she read my palm; it was very uplifting and made me feel much better about things. But she did say something about you. She said I should warn you to be careful, that there was danger."

Stella almost laughed out loud. Her mother was 24 hours too late. She decided not to mention it.

Sheila prattled on. "Anyway, I'm glad you'll be going home soon, dear. We'll see each other then. In the meantime, I better go. Daphne's waving at me. And be careful. I know Barbara loved Venice, but it always sounded a bit unsavory to me."

"I'll be careful. 'Bye, mum."

They hung up. Stella appreciated her mother's concern; the woman wasn't totally wrong. She'd like to know who'd attacked her and Olivia and who'd murdered Andrea and why before she left, but it might not be possible. Nigel's brother's drowning and Aunt Barb's trip and fall down the stairs were on Stella's suspicious radar, but what could she do about it? If she and Olivia could figure out what the dream Mothers meant by reading the diaries, maybe it would solve *something*. Stella picked up the Sergeant's business card from where she'd placed it on the credenza after he and Officer Baker left, looked at the phone number, then put it back. She could always give him a call for an update before she left. The stove timer dinged. Dinner was ready. Stella quickly finished drying off with the towel she'd wrapped around herself, let the water out of the bath tub, and put on a pair of pajamas.

She fished out her little black book from the beach bag and made catch-up entries while she ate the quiche, including the possibility that one of the tenants was the culprit. Carol worked long and hard hours; Liz worked even more hours when you added her acting schedule to the waitressing job. Greg could do with a tune-up in the personality department, but that didn't necessarily make him a murderer. Sam was an emotional softie and genuinely distraught over Andrea's death, plus Stella didn't personally feel any hostility from him. Still, that didn't let him entirely off the hook.

Gary Edwards in the house next door had seemed a little strange dolled up in a surgical outfit for an operation on his surfboard when she first met him, but he'd behaved normally at Aunt Barb's funeral. So what if he lived with his mother? Stella might have to live with hers for a while when she went back. She couldn't rule him out, though. Or Cindy and her little dog, Percy, even if they were friendly enough. Stella still hadn't met the other tenant in the front building. Carol had told her he not only worked as an orderly at the VA hospital, but was also going to school full-time. Plus, he had a girlfriend in West LA. Rent was due soon, but since Harry Bernstein had told her everyone paid in directly to her aunt's account, she still might not meet him.

It was quite late by the time she finished her notes. Mr. Velvet was asleep in the armchair. Stella took her dinner dishes into the kitchen and washed them, then made sure the front and back doors were securely locked. She went into the bedroom, turning lights out as she walked through the apartment, and pulled down the bed. Before hopping into it, Stella turned and closed the window shades. She didn't notice someone watching her. Sergeant Martinez sat in an unmarked car parked in the shadows of the alley behind Vi and Edna's house.

CHAPTER 29

Stella picked up one of the little black books at random from the short stack and spent an hour reading from it while she at her breakfast the next morning. She couldn't wait for Olivia to come and stay for the weekend. There was a lot to get through and it was slow going. Besides her aunt not fully dating all the entries, the writing was sometimes neat, sometimes scribbled, and often written in different color inks depending on which pen she had on hand, Stella supposed.

She skimmed over several pages where Barbara talked about friends, the names of which Stella didn't recognize, except Carol. Apparently the two women often took walks along the beach if Carol got home from work early enough before it got dark, sometimes stopping for a frozen yogurt on Main Street on the way back. The neighbors also went to the movies together occasionally. Stella read about such an outing with Gary Ewards, Liz, Carol, and Cindy going to the cineplex in the Marina after an afternoon of swimming and boogie-board surfing. Auntie Barb had written that they'd had trouble getting up from their seats when the film ended because they were exhausted from their bodies being slammed into the sand by the force of the waves. They'd all started laughing at their collected pain of banged up knees and elbows.

Stella flipped through a few more pages detailing shopping lists, car repairs, Mr. Velvet's vet bill and who was late with the rent, but stopped at a quote from David Thoreau: *The question is not what you look at, but what do you see?*

She sat pondering that when Mr. Bernstein rang. He was horrified to hear about her night in the basement.

"Good God! Are you alright? Did you file a police report?"

She assured him she had.

"Good. We'll need a copy of that for the court This whole thing's taken a nasty turn. And now I'm beginning to think... that, that so-called accident...poor Barb!" Stella heard a sob in his voice. He sounded really shaken, then got control of himself. "Listen, if the cops want to contact me I'm fine with that. I want to help in any way I can. What's the name and phone number of the officers you spoke to?"

So he had the same doubts she did. Stella picked up Martinez's and Baker's cards from beside the phone and read them off to Harry.

"Good. I might give them a call. Anything else I should know?"

She told him about Ray's son dropping by. Harry was disappointed she didn't have Scott's address or phone number, but glad she'd told the police about him. "They might track him down," he said. "I'll ask them first."

She heard him take a deep breath over the phone. "Let me bring you up to date on my end. The Notary Public's no longer active. According to the State of California and the National Notary Association, she died last year. Cancer. So this recent will is really suspicious. We can't ask her about

Gabriel Charities or who represented them when she notarized the document in 1991, or this 1993 one, which we know didn't happen, but we have to prove it to the court. No new or updated phone number or address for Gabriel Charities as yet, but we'll keep looking. I've hired a private investigator to dig deeper. Now you've told me about Ray's son I'll put him onto that, too, after I ask the police. This is all going towards filing an objection to that will with the court. We'll see who we can flush out, but whoever it is...I think they're getting desperate. You be careful now, very careful," he warned.

"I will, Harry," she promised. "My friend, Olivia, is coming to stay for the weekend."

"Good. I'm sure she'll be on the alert after getting banged up. The pair of you have to be extremely careful. That's about it for now, but on another note, remember to give me any mail that comes to your aunt. You can ditch the ads and the Penny Saver, anything along those lines."

Stella checked the kitchen wall clock; the mail should be here by now. "Okay. 'Bye." They rang off.

Stella stood outside the front building of *Billy's* a few moments later, two envelopes in one hand, watching the sun sparkling on top of the waves like an Impressionist's painting. It was lovely here if you discounted some of the events that had occurred, she decided. But didn't those things happen everywhere, and more frequently it seemed nowadays? A man approached from the Boardwalk and stood on the other side of the white picket fence.

"Excuse me," he called to her. He wore a Dr. Seuss hat and carried a piece of 2x4 in his hand.

Stella waited, uncertain what might be on his mind, but kept her eye on the piece of wood. What if he was violent?

What if he was the one who had attacked her and Olivia the night before last?

He made a little bow. "I apologize for any offense I've given you. I apologize on behalf of all men to you as a woman for anything I've said or done that may have hurt or offended you in any way. Will you accept my apology?"

Wow! On behalf of all men? How could she refuse? Brian sprang to mind.

"Umm," she hesitated. Not on behalf of *all* men; just this one, a complete stranger. Maybe. In spite of his strange appearance, he seemed harmless enough. And there were other people around, jogging, strolling or roller-skating along the Boardwalk. "Okay," she replied nervously.

"One more thing," the strange man said. "Would you take care of this for me?" He held out the piece of 2x4.

Stella walked towards the fence for a closer look. Something was carved into what he held. An Arabic figure maybe?

"Thanks." He shoved the piece of wood into her hands, turned away and walked across the beach.

"What did Cat in the Hat want?" Carol came from the direction of the mini-mart with a candy bar in her hand and opened the gate.

Stella stood aside to let her into the yard. "He gave me this," she held the 2x4 out. "Something's carved there, but I can't read it."

Carol closed the gate behind her, put the candy bar in her jacket pocket, and peered closely. "Hold it the other way."

Stella turned it sideways. "Maybe it's a foreign code."

Carol smiled. "I guess that could be code. It's got the number '13' carved into it."

"He gave me his damn doorpost!" Stella walked over to a tub of roses and stuck the 2x4 into it. She repeated what the man had said to her as they watched him join a circle of people sitting cross-legged on the sand.

"Are they meditating?"

Carol looked amused. "Hardly. That's the Venice chapter of C.A. having their weekly meeting."

"C.A?"

"Cocaine Anonymous. Wealthier people move into the neighborhood, the bigger the circle gets."

Just then Gary Edwards came out of his house accompanied by the mailman.

His mother, wearing shorts and ballet flats, her white hair done up in a bun, followed. "Thank, you John," she called, as the two men walked to their gate and Gary opened it to let the mailman out onto the Boardwalk.

Mrs. Edwards spied Carol and Stella. "It's my birthday today. He came in to play 'Happy Birthday' on our piano. Wasn't that sweet of him?" she called over.

John hitched his mailbag higher on his shoulder and turned to wave goodbye before walking off to his next delivery. They all waved back.

Mrs. Edwards turned to Carol and Stella. "We're having cake. Come in and join us."

Cake for lunch? Why not? She stuffed the two envelopes into her jeans pocket.

"The Edwards' house is three years older than our place," Carol told her as they detoured out of *Billy's* front yard and into the Edwards's. "Built in 1907. It's a beach house, railway carriage style with the rooms running into each other like our apartments. Mrs. Edwards bought it after the war when property was cheap because Venice was getting run-down by then, and people were moving to new houses in the suburbs. Gary grew up on the beach."

"Thanks for filling me in."

Inside the living room Bill Craven sat on a settee that certainly looked as if it had been there since the 1940s. Stella looked around to see if Vi and Edna were on site, but the only other visitor was Liz in her restaurant uniform, who jumped up from a nearby wing chair as Stella and Carol entered. Mrs. Edwards sat by the empty fireplace in another easy chair, which not only afforded her a complete view of the living room, but out of the window to the Boardwalk.

"I have to get going, got to go to work early today. Double shift. We're short-staffed. Thanks for the cake, and Happy Birthday, Mrs. E." Liz bent down and kissed the old lady's cheek.

"Thank you, dear."

"I'll see you out." Gary opened the front door again and walked Liz to the front gate. Stella noted he looked disappointed that she was leaving.

"Liz works at that swanky new restaurant just off of the Boardwalk," Mrs. Edwards said. "I think they're taking advantage of her. She's a hard worker." She flapped a well-manicured hand. "Sit down, girls. I've been wanting to meet you," she told Stella, directing both women to a second couch by a coffee table littered with crumb-smeared paper plates and plastic forks. "I'm sorry to have missed your aunt's funeral, but I was in the hospital. Or did they send me home that particular day? Or was it the day after?" she thought for a nanosecond, then sighed and shook her head as she threw her hands in the air. "Can't remember! This is Bill Craven, an old Venice neighbor."

"We've already met," Stella said, as Bill smiled and waggled his fingers in a little wave.

"Oh, when was that? He just got here, when was it Bill– yesterday morning?" Gary's mother had a languid, fluttery way of talking, like women from the1930s when they were referred to as girls until they were in their eighties.

"Early yesterday morning, very early, more like the middle of the night." Bill chuckled, "I rescued Stella and her friend from the basement."

"What?" Mrs. Edwards looked puzzled.

Bill started to explain just as Gary came back into the room. He stood by the piano, listening, then sat down on the piano stool facing the group as Stella added a few particulars.

"Did any of you hear or see anything?" she asked as Carol, Gary and his mother looked alarmed. "It would have been late at night."

"I'm out like a light these days on my medication," Mrs. Edwards told her. "My head hits the pillow early and I don't wake up until the sun streams in the window and it's time for my morning medication. Which actually makes me sleepy most of the day," she added thoughtfully.

"I get so tired after gardening, I can barely manage to eat dinner and take a warm bath before I'm ready to crawl between the sheets," Carol said. "And I stay there until the alarm goes off. This is terrible, Stella."

"There's a lot of unsavory characters wandering around out there after dark these days, but the ocean's always lulled me to sleep so I never hear anything." Gary looked serious. "Perhaps it's the same person who murdered Andrea."

"Poor girl. I don't see what's wrong with a little flirting." Mrs. Edwards smiled at Bill Craven as she said it.

Stella thought that might be a bit of an understatement, but was too polite to say so. Andrea's behavior was obviously not a state secret. *She could have pissed a lot of people off.* Stella wondered what time Gary went to bed, since it was quite late when she'd seen him outlined in the window that time soon after she arrived.

"Have the police found out who did it yet?" Carol asked.

"They released Sam. I haven't heard anything more," Gary replied.

"What about your lifeguard friends?"

"As of this morning, they haven't been told anything, either."

"Gary, cut these girls a slice of cake." Mrs. Ewards changed the subject. "I already ate a piece with the mailman," she confessed, "and a few other people, including Cindy, who brought that horrible little dog with her. Darn mutt lifted its leg against the coffee table, but Gary stopped it just in time." She smiled at her son. "And put on a fresh pot of coffee, too. Or would you prefer tea?" she asked Stella.

"Coffee's fine, thank you," she replied, settling in for the duration. The old lady's birthday was a chance to get to know her a little, and hopefully hear some gossip about the neighborhood, which might help her figure out what was going on.

"It's good to see you again, Bill," Carol said as Gary got up from his piano seat perch and went through the dining-room, where Stella could see the lesser half of a pink-frosted cake sitting on the table next to a stack of paper plates. He disappeared into the kitchen beyond where she heard the tap running as he filled the coffee maker with water. "How's Idaho?"

"A lot quieter than this," Bill nodded out the window towards the Boardwalk. "Ah, I see the Snake and Parrot Man's back." He strained for a better look. "Doesn't look like he has the python with him today."

He and Stella exchanged glances.

"What else did we miss?" Gary's mom asked, looking at him.

Stella explained about finding Monty and the impending motherhood. "Only now she's been renamed Minnie."

The old lady shivered. "Ugghh, I hate snakes."

"I think we found Greg's missing cat, too."

'I don't like cats, either," Mrs. Edwards stated.

Stella nodded. *No wonder Mr. Velvet uses her flowerbed as his personal pissoir.*

"You found Greg's cat? Where?" Gary came back to the living-room carrying two of the paper plates with large slices of cake on them. He handed one to Stella and one to Carol along with forks and napkins. "Want another piece of cake, Bill?"

"Oh, no." Bill patted his abdomen. "One was plenty."

Stella explained the bulge in Minnie's stomach. A debate followed as to whether they should tell Greg or not.

"He loved Hitler," Gary said, who was now handing round mugs of coffee.

"He has a right to know," Stella opined. "Even though it's only a suspicion."

"Then you tell him," Gary suggested.

Stella nodded. "All right, I will. Even though we can't prove it's Hitler. It's just a guess."

"A good guess," Carol said. "An educated guess."

Mrs. Edwards chimed in. "You'd need an autopsy for real proof."

"We know that's not going to happen," Gary told his mother as he sat back down on the piano stool, then turned towards Stella. "I've got a spare lock you can have for the basement door if that helps."

"That's very nice of you. Thanks."

"The tenants need to get into their stuff they store down there, bikes and surfboards and things," Carol pointed out. "Each apartment dweller would need a key."

"It already comes with two keys," Gary countered. "You just need to get a few more made."

"That's doable." Stella would have to run this small expense past Harry Bernstein, but surely he'd agree in light of things.

"Those mesh vents need fixing. I've got a leftover roll of fine wire mesh. I can cut some pieces off and hammer them in place," Carol offered. "That would be a simple job, Keep the cats out of there."

"And other critters," Bill Craven added. "I saw a possum sauntering across Speedway last night. She came from your direction," he nodded at Mrs. Edwards, "and headed off down the alley."

"How'd you know it was a she?" Gary demanded.

"Babies on her back, clinging for dear life."

In light of recent events, Stella thought this was a poor choice of words. Instead, she wondered aloud at the abundance of wildlife in such a big city.

"Are you kidding, the possums hang out with the cats at night," Carol told her. "I've stood on the back porch and watched Mr. Velvet down in the garden, sitting on the edge of the pond with his tail dangling in the water. He gently swishes it back and forth enticing the curious goldfish. I bet there's cat versions of a barbecue going on in the middle of the night. Our pets are partying down there on the patio."

"I've even seen raccoons eating leftover pizza from the Boardwalk trash cans after dark," Gary added. Mrs. Edwards nodded in agreement.

While everyone was highly amused by animals' antics when humans weren't around, Stella cut short her vision of raccoons strolling down the Boardwalk and dining out. Maybe everyone didn't always go to bed as early and sleep as soundly as they claimed.

CHAPTER 30

Carol was finishing up her slice in large bites. "The cake's very good, Mrs. E."

"Gary baked it for me." Mrs. Edwards cast a loving look at her son. "From one of my old recipes."

Stella liked the cake part, but thought the frosting sickly sweet. She tried to scrape some of it off without anyone noticing, managing to leave a few pink smears on the plate as she washed the last bite down with coffee. Gary gathered up the plates as soon as she and Carol had finished, and disappeared them into the kitchen.

"My husband liked cake. I used to bake every week. In those days we made everything from scratch. During the war some things were rationed. We had this yellow powder to mix into lard. Oleo margarine they called it. Much cheaper than butter."

Stella wondered if she'd just eaten sugared lard colored pink with red food dye; the thought made her queasy so she banished it from her mind. *I don't want to start throwing up again. It was bad enough after Aunt Barb's funeral.*

Carol noticed the time on the mantle clock and stood up. "I'd love to stay, but I better get going back to work. I just came home for a quick lunch and a cup of coffee, but this was much better. A nice surprise." She went over and gave Gary's mother a peck on the cheek. "Happy Birthday, Mrs. E."

"Thank you, dear." The old lady glanced out of the window at the metallic sound of the front gate being unlatched. "Oh, look, here comes Greg."

Carol gave Stella a meaningful glance, then beat a hasty retreat, saying a quick "Hi," to Greg on the way out.

Greg took the news that Hitler was possibly dead, probably dead, very badly. He was sobbing when Stella finally left. Bill Craven was right behind her.

"I'm going for a walk on the beach," she told him.

"Mind if I join you?"

"Not at all."

As they walked across the sand, Stella realized he must know about the history of the neighborhood just as well or perhaps even better than Mrs. Edwards, despite having been away at sea for years at a time after he grew up.

When they reached the tideline. Stella slipped her sandals off so the edge of the incoming waves could wash over her toes. After picking them up and holding them with one hand, she took a deep breath and exhaled.

"I love the smell of the sea, the saltiness of it, the fishyness, even the smell of seaweed–before it dries," she added. "I was born by the ocean. The hospital faced the sea."

Bill chuckled. "Me, too. I was born in Santa Monica." He kept his shoes on and stayed on the dry sand as they walked south towards Venice Pier.

"Mrs. Edwards was comforting Greg like she'd known him for a long time. Has she?" Stella wanted to know.

Bill shrugged. "A few years. His mother used to live in that apartment he's occupying now. She and Mrs. E. were friends. They played cards and drank afternoon cocktails together. Greg moved in after his mother died. I gather it was less expensive to live there than his apartment in Hollywood."

"What about Gary? Did he ever live anywhere else?"

"Nope. Never left home." Bill's lip curled slightly. "Never worked, either. Gary lives off his mother's income."

"That must be difficult."

Bill shrugged. "She owns property."

His blue eyes kept straying towards the horizon now as they walked and talked. "My mom died when I was fourteen, A couple of years later, I finally ditched high school permanently and joined the Navy. Although I'd be gone for a year or two at a time, I'd always come back to visit Aunt Vi and Edna. Mom and I had lived with them after my step-dad died." He smiled ruefully. "Vi and Edna made an interesting pair of mother substitutes, but they were always good to me."

Stella nodded. She bet they were, remembering what Carol had said about them preferring males over females. "How's the quest for a rest home going?"

"I haven't told them yet," he admitted as they made a detour around two boys throwing a football back and forth at the edge of the waves. "They think I'm moving back in."

"Would you?"

"I might have to for a while. Edna's losing her sight and Vi needs a hip replacement. Neither of them trust having caregivers in the house. They think strangers will steal things. Not that they have much of anything to steal. Their furniture's ancient compared to the Edwards's, although there are a few more recent pieces they've added." He laughed. "I noticed a couple of additions in the living room, two easy chairs circa 1970, horrible avocado green upholstery. Vi told me Gary goes round the neighborhood the night before trash collection when everyone puts out their trash cans as well as what they don't want anymore. He got them a partial set of dishes so they could throw out the cracked ones in use since Rome was sacked. Or, at least, as long as I remember." He chuckled again, then turned somber.

"They'd never been used to having much money as young women, then the Depression came, and everyone was making do. It's been like that for them most of their lives. There was some respite when Mom married. Apart from a little social security and a few government bonds, their wealth's tied up in two-thirds of the house." He sighed. "It'll have to be sold for them to go into a nursing home."

"Who owns the other third of the property?"

"You're looking at him."

"Quite a lot of difficult decisions to be made then."

"Mmnn."

Stella silently wondered how much longer a pair of ninety-somethings in declining health could live. "Private nursing homes in the UK can be quite expensive," she told Bill. "Although most people qualify for ones under the National Health system."

"None of that here. They're ridiculously expensive," he replied. "Especially in California. And neither of the old dears have anything like a long-term health insurance policy. By the time the powers-that-be dreamed those up, both Vi and Edna were too old to be able to get one. Not that they could've afforded the premiums," he added.

Stella thought of her mother and Jim, and their holiday in Spain being interrupted by Jim's back accident while snorkeling. Sheila had complained mainly about having their fun being interrupted rather than worrying about the price of his medical care. For all its opulence and opportunities, America was a wonderful place she thought, but the Europeans took better care of people's basic needs.

They walked on in silence for a while. It was low tide and they frequently dodged clumps of seaweed left on the shoreline as they neared the pier.

"It's a good thing I didn't bring the dog with me." Bill was looking at the bank of signs advising what you could and couldn't do after they walked away from the sea and up to the Boardwalk. "He used to love to run across the beach and retrieve his ball or a stick I'd throw into the ocean for him. Now dogs on the beach are being banned. It's getting so a person can hardly live anymore."

Stella, meanwhile, observed how little people were paying attention to the rules. They were riding their bikes or roller-blading along the Boardwalk, flicking lighted cigarette stubs aside in spite of many people walking barefoot, and tossing empty Styrofoam cups–or worse, beer bottles–at the trash cans instead of into them. A golden retriever was defecating in the sand as they walked past him in spite of any municipal code. *Perhaps that's why rules were necessary–to encourage people to care for and care about their environment.* Stella put her sandals back on.

"Oh, the pier's still closed." Bill was disappointed as they stood at an entrance barrier looking down the long walkway stretching out into the ocean.

"It's unsafe," a rollerblader, bare-chested with his folded shirt hanging down from where he'd tucked into his shorts waistband, stopped beside them. "City wanted to tear it down, but the residents stopped it. They've almost raised enough funds to restore it. Come back in a few years and you'll be able to fish off of it again." He skated away on Washington Boulevard, deftly weaving amongst cars looking for a parking spot.

"I better get back," Bill said. "Vi and Edna will be getting restless."

"Can't have that," Stella teased.

"Amen."

They turned to walk back along the Boardwalk.

"It's a lot more crowded down this end," Stella remarked as they weaved through people who'd stopped to listen to some musicians. "It's like a carnival with all the crowds."

Bill laughed. "It's always been a carnival; there's always been crowds. That was the intention, a place designed for people to come and have a good time. Leave their cares and worries behind in the city and enjoy the fresh sea air. A popular attraction on the original Venice Pier was called the Fun House."

He was quiet for a moment. "It started to decline badly after World War II. Buildings and rides were dismantled. The city had other plans. It was called Marina del Rey. The area was in decline for several years while that was in the works.

Property values went down so it became affordable for artists, musicians, creatives and bohemians of all types to live here. That's when my step-dad bought *Billy's.* He and Mom and the aunts had gone through tough times themselves when they couldn't afford rent, knew others in the same position since they and their friends worked the carnival attractions, so they kept rents low enough so people could have a place to live. Vi and Edna kept it up while I was away. Just because you were a little different from others or didn't have much money shouldn't mean you couldn't have shelter, a place to call home. I agreed. *Billy's* has always been full of artists an bohemians or hippies." He took a deep breath.

"I liked your aunt. She shared the same values and appreciated the neighborhood. She wasn't in it for a quick buck. That's why I sold it to her instead of someone else," he added. "I'm sorry to hear what happened. It's hard to believe she fell down those steps."

Yes, it is. "I don't know much about her," Stella admitted.

"Well, ask Carol. She was very close to your aunt. "At one time I even though they might be an item."

"What?"

"Oh, yes. After Carol's kids left home, she and her husband got divorced, then she changed her lifestyle. I believe she's now what you'd call a gay grandma."

"How long did they know each other?"

"Few years, I guess. Carol knew Barbara and her husband before they moved here. She recommended them to me as suitable tenants. Your aunt was a friendly gal. What they used to call 'a free spirit,' although I understand she was devoted to her husband." Bill paused for a moment, thinking. "Guess he was rather a free spirit himself. I didn't know them very well before he passed, but was told they'd been together for quite a while. But you must know all this."

"I don't," Stella admitted. She'd have to have a talk to Carol.

Nearing *Billy's*, they encountered Cindy walking her little dog, Percy. She hailed them. "Carol told me about what happened. Really freaked me out. Thank God you came along when you did," she said to Bill, who nodded.

"You live in one of the front apartments," Stella said. "My friend and I came home late. Did you hear us? Or anything?"

Cindy shook her head. "No. I close my blinds after the sun goes down and put my TV on, watch my programs for the rest of the evening, then turn in early. Percy does, too. He sleeps on the pillow right next to me. Neither of us is a late-night person, are we?" She made baby talk noises to the p'doodle, who peered up at her with adoring eyes, his little pink tongue hanging out as he panted. "Sometimes his snoring wakes me up, but usually we're both out cold until morning."

"He doesn't bark in the middle of the night if someone comes in the front gate?" Bill asked.

"Oh, no. The Boardwalk's all white noise to him. Me, too. Plus, the old apartments are remarkably soundproof. Unless you have the windows open, and I don't at night, being on the ground floor. Don't want some anyone climbing in while I'm asleep."

"Of course not. Well, enjoy your walk," Stella said, and turned to go.

"I'll be more vigilant, keep an ear open and monitor the front gate for any strangers coming or going," Cindy called after her. "We're all here for you, Stella."

"Thanks," she replied. "Oh, one thing I've been meaning to ask you, Cindy. Did you get an upset stomach after my aunt's funeral party?"

"Did I ever," Cindy was rueful. "It always happens when I drink champagne. You'd think I'd spent enough time in my life vomiting from it by now, but, no, I obviously haven't learned my lesson yet; or, hadn't, rather. I think I've finally accepted the fact my system doesn't like bubbles. Why? Did others get ill?"

"Carol told me they did."

Cindy shrugged. "I didn't hear anyone else complaining. Greg told me he thought the sausage on the pizza tasted funny when he took a bite, so he didn't finish eating it, but that was about it."

"Okay." Stella watched her and Percy disappear into the crowd, then she and Bill walked on.

"Sounds like Barbara had quite a send-off."

"Oh, she did." Stella told him about the sushi and champagne boat ride and her aunt's ascent into the night sky to the strains of Led Zeppelin.

He started laughing. "That sounds just like something she'd plan. I'm sorry I missed it. He stopped laughing. "Although I'm sorry she died in the first place. A slip and fall. So unlike her." He shook his head sorrowfully.

"I have my doubts," Stella confided. "But the cops thought it was an accident and the medical examiner didn't have a different finding."

Bill sighed. "Accidents do happen."

"You knew both my aunt and her husband."

"Just briefly, before Ray died as I mentioned. We weren't close friends, but I knew them both a bit, yes. Then after Ray went, I got to know your aunt better."

"Did Ray ever mention his son? Or did Barbara say anything about him after Ray died?

"No. Neither of them said anything that I remember."

Stella though it was a shame that strangers had known more about Barbara Smith's life than her own family. She'd ask her mother about it the next time they met in person. It wasn't a subject one could have an in-depth conversation about over a transatlantic phone call.

They reached *Billy's* and parted. Craven told Stella to be careful, that he'd keep an eye out for what was going on, which made her feel better about her neighbors and their neighborhood. She walked through to the garden and encountered Greg standing on the far side of the Norfolk pine, contemplating something in the space between the back building and the Edwards' fence.

"Hitler used to hang out here," he said. "It was his sunny spot for an afternoon nap, by the broken mesh vents. It must've been where the python got him. *If* he got him. I'm not ready to give up on the thought that he was not the bulge in that snake's stomach. It could have been a possum. Hitler could be out and about in the neighborhood for a few days, catting around, dining out. He's been known to do that before. People feed him. He's a con artist. Since he looks all white and fluffy, people think he's either lost his way, that he's been abandoned, or maybe his carers have brought a puppy home, that he doesn't like dogs and is looking for new accommodation. Of course, he disappears after a quick pet and a hearty meal. The scoundrel," Greg ended affectionately.

People always think their kids are innocent.

"He hissed at me from the moment I arrived," Stella said. "I understand he used to scratch people, too. And pick fights with the other tenants' cats."

"It's true, he could be a bad boy. I suppose Carol told you that. Just because he clawed her once or twice." Greg wasn't about to let go of his fond cat memories.

And beat up her cat, Pumpkin, to the tune of two hundred dollars in vet bills. But Stella wanted to be kind. After all, the guy was missing a pet he loved. "Perhaps he will turn up. In the meantime, is that scrap lumber from building the stairs?" She nodded at a pile of wooden planks by the vents. Carol hadn't used much of it for the Hecate's Hags bonfire.

"Yeah, from rebuilding the back stairs for the front building, too. I was thinking I could build a gate to put at each end of the garden. That way strangers couldn't walk through so easily. I think we'd all feel a bit safer. What do you think? If there's enough wood you'd just have to pay for my labor."

"That sounds like a good idea, Greg, but I'm afraid it's not up to me. My aunt's estate is in the hands of her lawyer, he's the executor. It'd have to be run by him."

"What? Does that mean I'm not going to be able to get reimbursed for fixing the back steps now?" Greg burst out. "Barbara and I had an agreement to deduct costs and labor from the rent and you indicated it was okay."

"And it is. I gave the receipt from the lumber yard and your bill for labor, along with the note Aunt Barb had made about the agreement between the two of you, to her lawyer. He said it was fine. The agreement's going to be honored. You don't have to worry about it. And this new idea about the gates, I'll mention that I think it's a good idea. Can you estimate how much it would cost for your labor and write it down so I can send it to him?"

"Okay," Greg agreed, going back to perusing the pile of lumber.

Stella remembered the mail in her pocket and pulled it out smoothing the envelopes which had become a little crumpled after sitting on the Edwards' sofa. "And sooner rather than later would be best. In fact, if you can give me a ballpark figure now, I'll call and let him know."

Greg thought for a moment, then pulled a pen out of his pocket and reached for one of the envelopes. She handed it to him and he scribbled a figure down before handing it back.

"There. I've included the cost for nails."

CHAPTER 31

Stella spent the rest of the afternoon cleaning and tidying in preparation for Olivia's upcoming visit. Mr. Velvet sat and watched from the comfort of the armchair. She was putting the broom away in the kitchen cupboard, when Carol knocked on the back door.

"Since I set up the lights on the back porch as well as down on the patio when I started cultivating the garden, I switch them on from inside my kitchen."

"I wondered how they functioned," Stella replied.

"And since they're on my electricity bill, I turn them off when I go to bed."

Ergo no light when Aunt Barb was out there and fell. Or was pushed.

"But with that attack on you and your friend, I'll leave them on all night so it's not so dark out there."

"Thank you, I think that's wise. Then we can all feel a bit safer." Stella held the door open wider. "I was about to have a cup of tea. Would you like one?"

"Yes, I would."

"Come in." Stella put the kettle on and motioned Carol into the back room. "Let's sit on the settee." Since Carol had told her "everyone's got food poisoning," when it was turning out that such might not be the case, Stella wanted some clarification on that issue, too.

Carol defended her statement. "Everybody was telling me they didn't feel well the next day. Cindy had been throwing up, Greg had a belly ache, Liz said she had a very bad headache, two of Barbara's friends both said they felt ill, and you were on the bathroom floor all night."

"Maybe we all drank too much."

Carol shrugged. "Maybe. I did mention Gary and I were all right."

While Stella was mulling this over, Carol changed the subject.

"Did you tell Greg what you think happened to his cat? How's he doing?"

"He's in denial."

Carol nodded. "Not surprising. But the upside to Hitler's demise is maybe *my* cat will come out of the closet where she's been hiding ever since he attacked her and be able to stroll around the garden without fear."

"He's thinking about building gates so people won't be able to access the property so easily, although you'd think the fence and the gate in front would be enough to keep people from wandering in from the Boardwalk."

"You might need a "Keep Out" sign, too," Carol suggested. "Not that that would deter some idiots."

At the sound of the tea kettle whistle, Stella jumped up and went into the kitchen. "Regular black tea okay, or would you prefer something herbal?" she called out.

"Regular's fine," Carol shouted back.

Stella brought in a tea tray containing two mugs and the teapot, and put it down on a small side table. "I've brought some milk and sugar, too, in case you take it."

"Not for me."

Stella was about to sit down when she glanced out of the window and frowned. *Not him!*

"What is it?" Carol stood up and looked out of the window, too. "What are you looking at?"

"That building on the other side of the parking lot, the beige one that fronts Brooks Avenue and goes back to the alley."

"Oh, the youth hostel. It used to be a regular apartment building before it changed hands. That place is a nuisance at times. You have a lot of people coming and going; it's a cheap vacation place to stay for a couple of days. Barbara used to complain when it got too rowdy over there."

"Did she now." Stella thought that sounded rather out of character for her aunt.

"It's quiet at the moment. I don't see anyone over there," Carol said.

Stella turned from the window, sat down, and poured them both mugs of tea. She didn't see anyone over there, either, now. But she had seen Nigel exit the hostel and walk off down the street zipping something into his backpack.

CHAPTER 32

Stella didn't have a chance to ask Carol about her friendship with Aunt Barb, or Ray. Carol drank her tea, then left, saying she had to babysit her grandchildren. After she'd gone, Stella defrosted a salmon fillet under the kitchen tap, then poached it for a quick dinner with some salad. She shared the fish with Mr. Velvet, who then took off for a nocturnal stroll while she cleared the dishes and had a bath.

Stella put on one of Aunt Barbara's nightdresses, then sat down at the dining-room table with her journal, making notes to try and clear her mind.

Why was Nigel still around? What was he doing at the youth hostel?

She reached for the phone and dialed her home number. It was the middle of the night in the UK.

"Yeah?" a sleepy voice answered

"Brian, it's me."

"Stella, I've been worried about you!" Now he sounded wide-awake.

"That's nice, I'm fine, but I only have a moment." She didn't want to go into a lengthy explanation on her end, so she asked a direct question to which she hoped he'd give a short answer. "Where's Nigel?"

"What? Nigel? He's still in LA."

"Why?"

"He had to wait for the body to be released, and then have his brother cremated so he could bring him back to England. We're having the funeral here next week. Why do you want to know? I thought you threw Nigel out."

"I did, but I just saw him at the youth hostel near here."

"That's the last place Neville stayed. They had his passport in their safe. Nigel needed it to sign some final documents."

"That explains it, then. Thanks."

"Wait, wait, wait, you and I have to sort things out. When are you coming back?"

"No idea. There's a lot to sort out here, too. In fact I'm right in the middle of a big sort-out as we speak. I can only do so much at one time. I'll let you know later. Gotta go, 'Bye." And she hung up.

Now that she'd answered her own questions about her ex-lover's current paramour and what he was still doing in Venice, Stella jotted down the events of the day and the offers of help she'd received. That done, she now felt better about her neighbors and ready for bed. Only she wasn't tired, just tense. The brief phone call with Brian had unnerved her. In spite of being awakened in the middle of the night, he had sounded good, loving even. A voice from home. *While I'm just stuck here in this liminal space.* It wasn't that Stella felt she was at the other end of the world, just on the other side of it in a kind of no man's land with unknown shadows all around. Knowing Olivia would be there the following day calmed her down, as did the thoughts of supportive neighbors, but Stella needed something to do. Now. Watching television or reading one of her aunt's many novels lining the wall shelf wouldn't be enough of a distraction to quieten down some nagging thoughts at the back of her mind that she couldn't quite reach. Her eyes settled on the little stack of Aunt Barb's diaries from the past three years set aside for a weekend of reading by her and Olivia. Deciding to follow the Night Mother's advice in her dream to "read the little black book," she chose one at random, then settled down with it in the faded armchair that Mr. Velvet frequented. *No wonder he likes it; this old chair is lumpy but comfy.*

Stella flipped through the pages of her aunt's journal dated 1990 until an entry caught her eye.

Lovely after-party at Liz's showcase last night. She's such a good actress. Met a young attorney friend of hers and we had an interesting chat. I've been wondering what to do now Ray's gone and I've got his life insurance money, etc. I've been talking to Bill Craven about buying the apartment building. The attorney said I should protect my assets. Be wise to have my own will. Can type one up myself using boilerplate language from any sample will book, then get it notarized. Made it sound easy enough. He'll help. Gave me his phone number.

A few days later, and a few pages on, there was another entry, splashed with what might have been tears.

Ray's sudden passing forces me to be practical. Got a will book from the library and typed something up from one of their samples. I feel I'm too young for this, but then so was my darling Ray. I have to take charge and take care of things. Be sensible. Be normal. What a strange feeling!

Her aunt then rambled on for several pages ranting about how unfair it was that life interrupted when a person was busy having fun. Stella began to get an inkling why her mother felt the way she did about her sister. "Barbara's dark side," Sheila had vaguely referred to it once, although Stella thought as she read on that her mother had got it wrong about her sister. If anything, Barbara was too light; she floated through life taking it as it came instead of plotting a route to how it should be. Bill Craven was right. She'd been a free spirit. But at least she'd hand-numbered this diary's pages at the top outer corner as she wrote.

Stella came to an update on page 114.

Called the lawyer. I told him I want to leave my assets to charity. He said type up a list. We agreed he'll stop by after work next week with the name of a notary public for me. He's leaving his current firm.

Perhaps that was why her aunt hadn't mentioned it. Stella turned more pages wondering what had happened to the typewriter as she quickly looked for more will references. She and Olivia could read about what else her aunt was up to later on as well, as conduct a more thorough search of her aunt's belongings in the cupboards.

Stella finally found an entry that Barbara had come up with the name of Gabriel for "Gabriel Charities," after Carol's first grandson. It was an umbrella name that would have a list all the non-profits underneath it that she'd like to donate any money left-over to after her death. She agreed with the attorney that it was easier if she put down one overall charitable name in the will, then compiled a list of individual places she wanted to support under the umbrella on a separate piece of paper. That way names could be added and subtracted as the years went by or as she changed her mind.

An excellent idea; then I won't have to keep making adden-dums to the will itself, Aunt Barb had written. The little black book contained a rough list of places she'd like to leave money to if there was any left at the end of her life: mostly private animal charities, including those rescuing marine life, as well as groups saving cats and dogs from being killed if they weren't adopted in a timely fashion from the county and municipal shelters; various musician's union organizations; outfits that helped women and children, sent inner city kids to summer camp, provided scholarships for students and a local arbore-tum that provided seedling trees for planting to beautify Los Angeles.

Stella turned a few more pages and read: *All done and dusted! Just got to take the will to this Notary Public he recom-mended. After that, I can stick the document in the filing cabinet with the list of non-profit type groups clipped to it under the Gabriel Charities header.*

Stella wondered if Carol knew Barbara had used the name of her grandson. In their conversations, Carol hadn't men-tioned anything. Stella also wondered if the list had ever been typed up. She hadn't seen a copy attached to the back of that first will. Stella sat and thought about it. Anyone could type up their will. It wasn't illegal or necessarily fraudulent. She'd noticed a few Do-It-Yourself books in the bookstore on the Boardwalk when she'd faxed the document to Harry Bernstein. Aunt Barb was in her late forties when the will had been drawn up and obviously didn't expect to die so soon. Plus, she didn't actually own an apartment building then. Gabriel's Charities was a made-up name, not a bona fide registered charity that was clear. But was it legal? Barbara hadn't mentioned the attorney by name so far. Maybe she'd made a notation of it later. Stella flipped more pages, quickly glancing through until she reached the end of the journal, but there were no further entries on the subject.

At best, the entries showed an intention to create something real; at worst it could be construed as suspicious, if not a scam of some sort. But on whose part? Stella had trouble believing her aunt would be intentionally involved in something like that. The journal clearly showed Barbara intended to set up something for good, not to be fraudulent. The problem was, had it actually been done? Perhaps her aunt was only guilty of not following through, of not completing her intention to set up Gabriel Charities in a recognizable manner with a list. Maybe her aunt hadn't been remiss. Someone could have taken it at any time, let alone when Stella arrived back at *Billy's* after almost being run over in the supermarket parking lot. Harry Bernstein thought the same-worded will dated 1993 instead of 1990 that had just come to light wasn't Barbara's handiwork.

Stella now believed someone had been in the apartment, had searched the filing cabinet looking for something, maybe looked through the rest of the place when she'd been gone, although there'd been no actual evidence of it, apart from the door being ajar. Someone else was standing in the shadows? But who? The lawyer? Who was he? Where was he? Harry was having trouble tracking him down because they didn't know. But someone knew. She'd ask Carol tomorrow if she knew.

Stella stuck a Post-it on the front of the book and wrote down the page numbers she'd just read for easy reference at a glance. Harry Bernstein would need Barbara's entries as evidence to bolster his argument of fraud re the 1993 will. But she needed to find out more. Surely her aunt had ruminated about changing the will in favor of Stella? There must be something written down in one of other diaries, but which one?

It was late, but Stella still didn't feel ready for bed. In fact, now she was on the trail, she felt more wide awake than ever, just thirsty. She walked into the kitchen for a drink of water and filled a glass from the tap, drank it down standing by the sink, then refilled the glass to take back to the dining room with her.

The apartment building was very quiet. Stella heard a sound that didn't quite belong to the night after she turned off the tap. Her inner Viking went on the alert. Opening the back door quietly, she slipped out onto the porch to see if someone had come into the garden. Carol had left a string of lights on that dimly illuminated the patio below, but nobody was there and nothing moved in the shrubbery. Night clouds drifted in from the ocean, shadowing the landscape, veiling the rooftops. Diffused street light made the palm trees on the Boardwalk glow neon green. All was hushed and still except for the buoy and its mournful warning bleeps down by the breakwater and the constant sighing of the sea as it rolled onto the shore.

Stella went back inside, locked the back door securely, collected her drink of water, then sat down in the armchair again and picked up another book, glancing at pages until she came to an entry that caught her attention: Aunt Barb had written *I've changed my mind.*

CHAPTER 33

It was dated the week before Harry Bernstein had drawn up the new will on behalf of his client in Stella's favor. *Something funny's going on at the youth hostel next to the parking lot,* her aunt wrote. *There's always been a lot of coming and going ever since it changed from being a regular apartment building, but traffic in and out's increasing the past year. I need to get out my binoculars.*

Stella had a vision of her aunt peering through the living-room/bedroom's blinds and across the tops of parked cars on the parking lot into a room full of youth hostel bunk beds. But what did this have to do with a will? She turned some more pages.

I saw Liz over there. This morning I asked her about it and she said something regarding a friend from New York coming into town. I asked her why she didn't meet them at her place, or even invite them to stay with her, Liz explained they'd turned up unexpectedly and she didn't have time to clear up or clean beforehand. Her apartment was a mess. She's been so busy working, going to auditions and rehearsing for a play. Okay, I can understand that. People are a bit less critical if a man's apartment isn't all shipshape. Women have such pressures on them.

Stella found herself nodding in agreement. She'd had to sweep up sand more often than she liked recently; it somehow blew in invisibly on the breeze through an open door or window right into her late aunt's apartment. That was the price of living at the beach; a gritty feeling to your bare feet on the living-room floor. The thought of housework made Stella yawn. Suddenly, she felt tired. Whatever Auntie Barb had changed her mind about and why could wait until tomorrow. She got up and went into the bathroom to brush her teeth before going to bed.

Stella turned off the lights when she came out and padded barefoot through the darkened dining room. Noise from the open window made her turn her head. A figure clad from head to toe in black like a Ninja jumped in a crouch across from the pine tree, through the window, and landed momentarily on the dining table before launching itself at her, grabbing and punching in a surprise attack.

Despite the shock Stella once again revived her inner Viking and fought back as hard as she could, getting in some good licks of her own, but the person was taller than her. It was a losing battle when something came round her neck from behind and the assailant started pulling tighter and tighter. It became harder and harder to breathe. Stella could feel blood rushing to her head. She was about to pass out.

Suddenly, there was an unearthly scream and the noose around her neck loosened. Stella slumped to the floor on her knees. Mr. Velvet had jumped through the window, then onto the intruder's shoulders with an angry "Yeeoww" and dug his claws in deep, his teeth sinking into the assassin's neck through the woolen balaclava. The assailant reached for the little furry body and pulled, but paws scratched at his rubber-gloved wrists and hands as the animal held on for dear life, howling like a banshee and snapping the thin rubber into shreds with sharp little teeth as well as fully extended claws. The intruder finally got traction on the cat and threw him off. But Mr. Velvet wasn't done. He'd landed hard on the floor, but on all fours. Before the attacker could grab Stella again, the valiant little animal hurled himself at the black-jeaned legs and hung on, biting and clawing through the cloth as he growled at full pitch. The assailant swatted at him, but Mr. Velvet was fast. And furious. He'd sunk his teeth in at the person's ankles, then the knees and then–the coup de grace: Mr. Velvet went for the crotch. There is nothing more painful than an animal's sharp claws sinking in deep, no matter how small the animal might be. It's the cut of a thousand knives, although only ten in this case to be accurate. Still, it was more than enough.

"AAAarrgggghhh," roared balaclava head bending over as the cat quickly jumped down to avoid getting hurt further, or, perhaps readying himself for an assault on a different part of the assailant's body.

Stella had never felt so light-headed in her life. Her head felt like it was made of cotton wool and she could hardly breath. Unable to get up, she managed to reach out, blindly groping around for some sort of traction until her fingers fastened onto one of her aunt's little black books she'd left on the armchair seat. Stella grabbed it and gave as mighty a whack as she could muster on her knees to that black-jeaned backside. The assailant stumbled away, wrenching the front door open and ran down the stairs.

"What the hell's going on?" The noise of fierce fighting and screaming had awakened Carol.

Stella finally caught enough breath and crawled towards the door which now sported a truly busted lock. Together they looked down the stairs where a scuffle had turned into a full-blown fight at the bottom. Sergeant Martinez and Officer Baker were wrestling with the intruder, who they finally subdued after he struck out with a vicious kick to the sergeant's forehead. Martinez wrenched the woolen balaclava off.

"Recognize him?" he shouted up the stairs to Stella.

"No," she croaked. And then she fainted.

CHAPTER 34

Paramedics were fussing over her when she came to. Someone had switched all the lights on and there was an oxygen mask on her face, which helped Stella breathe effortlessly and felt like heaven. *Am I dead?* Two handsome young men helped her sit up, then slowly stand, and finally deposited her gently in the armchair. *Oh, guess I'm not dead after all.* They told her no bones were broken, but she was badly bruised, suffering from shock, and had a bump on her forehead.

Carol appeared with a bag of frozen peas from her kitchen freezer. "Here, try this for the swelling."

One of the paramedics held the frozen packet while the other one removed the oxygen mask, then handed two tablets to Stella. "Pain meds. Do you have Tylenol or aspirin?"

She nodded, then felt dizzy and winced. "Ouch."

"These are extra strength. They'll last you for the next four hours. Then you can take whatever you have; just follow the directions on the bottle."

Stella swallowed the pain tablets down her sore throat with the glass of water that had miraculously not been knocked over and was still beside the armchair, then took the ice-cold peas the other paramedic held out and clamped the frozen bag to her forehead.

"Are you sure she doesn't need to go to the ER?" Carol hovered, concerned.

"No, really, I think I'll be okay," Stella answered. "I'd rather sit in this comfy chair than on a hard plastic one for hours in some hospital waiting room."

"You might want to check with your doctor tomorrow," the first paramedic advised. "The swelling's not bad, but they may suggest an x-ray or a CT scan just as a precaution."

"I can always call my doctor for you," Carol assured Stella. "I know you don't have one of your own." A whistle sounded from inside her apartment. "Ah, kettle's boiling. Be right back," she called over her shoulder as she walked out.

Mr. Velvet sat on the dining table watching everybody and everything as he licked all human-hands smell off and arranged his fur the way he liked it. Someone had bandaged his paw.

"He needs to go to the vet and get checked out too," the second paramedic told Stella. "I don't know what happened in here but it looks your kitty was assaulted as well as yourself. He needs a couple of stitches on his left ear and an x-ray for his leg to make sure it's not fractured. Plus, he's missing a few claw nails and I think he might have bruised ribs, but he wouldn't let me examine him for long."

"We can take him to my vet," Carol suggested coming back and handing a mug of hot ginger tea to Stella. "Here, drink this, it's got sugar in it. Good for shock." To the paramedic she said, "I'm surprised he let you examine him at all."

"I used to work at a vet's office," he replied. "I could tell the cat was in pain and injured the way he dragged himself across the floor. You're a sweetheart, aren't you," he cooed to Mr. Velvet, then added unnecessarily. "I like cats."

"He saved my life." Stella held the mug of tea in one hand and the frozen peas to her forehead with the other as she sipped the sweet brew.

"Brave boy," the paramedic said in admiration.

His partner finished packing medical equipment away in his bag. "I'll go help Max check out the perp. I hear he's got some deep lacerations on his face and neck, plus *someone* took a bite out of his ear. Bad kitty," he said *sotto voce*, then gave Mr. Velvet a wink as he went out the door.

Sergeant Martinez came clumping up the stairs. "How are we doing here?" He sported an adhesive bandage over a swollen cut from the assailant's kick to his forehead, but sounded very concerned about Stella.

In that moment, she had never been so glad to hear his voice.

"You managed to turn up awfully quick," Carol told him. "Thank God. I don't know what would have happened otherwise. That guy might have got away."

"Let's just say we were very close by," Martinez replied. "My partner and I saw a suspicious person enter your neighbor's yard, scramble up the tree and enter the open window. The cat came out of the bushes and jumped up into the branches after him. Darndest thing I ever saw. You were very lucky," he said to Stella. "We've had our eye on what's been happening around here for some time. I can't say much more about that since it's still an ongoing investigation at the moment." He turned to the paramedic who'd finished gently stroking Mr. Velvet and was shouldering his medical bag. "Aren't you taking her to the ER?"

"Why don't you ask me if I'm going since I'm sitting right here?" Stella knew she was being unreasonable, but she couldn't help herself. Apart from being angry at the attacker and in pain because the meds hadn't fully kicked in yet, she felt grumpy from lack of sleep and wanted to lash out at events beyond her control. Although she was grateful for his presence, the sergeant somehow always managed to rub her the wrong way. Then she felt contrite. He'd been there on the spot when needed and come to the rescue after all. Along with Mr. Velvet.

"She's not too badly hurt apart from the bump to the head." The paramedic lifted Stella's hand that held the bag of peas. "The swelling's going down. See." He turned to the officer. "How are you doing?"

"It's nothing." The sergeant gingerly touched his forehead. "I've had worse. Part of the job."

Martinez and the paramedic stepped out onto the landing to confer further as Stella drank the rest of her tea down and handed the empty mug to Carol.

"Thanks, that helped soothe my throat, which feels really sore."

Carol looked over at Mr. Velvet. "I can take him to my vet first thing in the morning if you like; I have a cat carrier. He's been roughed up, but I'm of the opinion that animals like to take care of themselves as much as they can."

"I do want him checked out," Stella agreed. "He might need pain meds as well as stitches. I don't want him to suffer. He's such a valiant little heart. He saved me." She got tears in her eyes at the thought of the little black cat's bravery and blew him a kiss. *What would I have done without you? I really would be dead.*

Mr. Velvet had positioned himself directly in front of the window and settled down on all fours, back legs slowly and carefully tucked under, his head gently laying across his front paws; his eyes became half-closed slits that slid towards the open front door as Sergeant Martinez re-entered.

"I need to ask you some questions," he said to Stella, almost apologetically. "If you're up to it." He noticed her blinking back tears and handed her a Kleenex from the box on the credenza. "Here."

"Thanks." Stella felt the meds starting to kick in. The cop really was being kind. And she was very thankful that he was so diligent at his job. "I understand. I'm okay; ask away. Carol, could I possibly have another cup of tea?"

"Certainly." She took the mug and went back to her own apartment, while the sergeant pulled out a chair from the dining-table and sat down facing Stella, snapping open his notebook and retrieving the pen in his shirt pocket. Mr. Velvet shifted his eyes to Martinez's back, but gradually closed them during the interview. After she came back with the fresh mug of tea, Carol pulled up a chair and sat down.

"Your assailant isn't talking," Martinez was saying. "Are you sure you haven't seen him before?"

"I don't think so," Stella replied, sipping the hot, sweet brew. Normally she didn't take sugar in any type of tea, herbal or black, but this tasted delicious in the moment.

"Do you want to take another look at him?"

"Not really."

"Since he was caught escaping from the act, it's not necessary, but it would help," the sergeant persisted. "We've got him in the patrol car outside. D'you think you'd be able to walk downstairs and take a look right now?"

"Just give me a minute." Stella's head was becoming clear enough to recognize that she was being interviewed in one of her aunt's old and faded rose-patterned shortie nighties that had definitely seen better days and should have been put in the rag pile long ago.

"All right," she told the police officer. "Carol, could you hand me the dressing gown from the back of the bathroom door? Thanks."

"I'd like you to take another look, too," Martinez said as the neighbor helped Stella into one of Aunt Barb's dressing gowns, mercifully of a much newer vintage than the nightdress. She'd also found a pair of slippers behind the bathroom door.

Carol nodded. "Of course. Anything to help put that SOB behind bars."

Amen, Stella echoed silently.

Both Carol and the sergeant helped steady her to stand and walk down the stairs to the police car parked outside. Speedway was blocked by several LAPD black-and-whites. Cops were in the alley, stationed by Brooks Avenue and standing around conversing in two's and three's. Lights were on upstairs at Vi and Edna's and Stella could see Bill Craven's silhouette looking out of one of the bedroom windows. Gary Edwards stood by his garden gate dressed in striped pajamas and what looked like an old smoking jacket while being interviewed by Officer Baker. All the lights were on in the youth hostel across the parking lot.

Stella looked closely at the man who sat handcuffed in the back seat of Martinez's patrol car. One ear was heavily bandaged and his face sported long strips of sticking plaster. Mr. Velvet had done a thorough job as warrior cat.

"How can I tell who it is? He practically looks like a freshly bandaged Egyptian mummy," she told Martinez, who stifled a laugh. Her medication was definitely working; Stella hardly felt any pain now.

"Do you recognize anything about him?"

"The sweater looks the same as the attacker wore. Are those my cat's claws caught in the wool?"

Martinez ducked his head down for a closer look at several opaque nails shining like tiny curved scimitars under the street light. "Think so. You have good eyesight, Ms. Maris." He signaled his partner over. "We need to bag those."

"He looks familiar, but I can't place where I've seen him before," Stella finally said turning away from her glaring assailant.

"Me, either," Carol told the officers after scrutinizing the man. "It's hard to recognize him even if you can see his eyes."

"Doesn't matter. We caught him running away from the scene. Book him, Baker," Martinez instructed his fellow officer, before he and Carol helped Stella back upstairs to her apartment.

"Tell me what happened." They sat back down in chairs they'd previously occupied. Sergeant Martinez re-opened his notebook. "Start at the beginning of your evening."

Stella told him she'd had dinner and a bath. "I wasn't very tired so I started to read one of my aunt's journals." She explained about the discrepancies in her aunt's wills. How Aunt Barb initially wanted money to go to her favorite charities, but something had made her change her mind later. "I was looking to see if she'd mentioned why in her diary."

"And did she?"

"I haven't found that part yet."

"We might need the diary as evidence, then."

I don't know about that. Stella was all for law and order but there was something about him that still rubbed her the wrong way in spite of his being so nice. She wasn't about to cave. Besides, there were some personal things about her family in those diaries she didn't want bantered around, especially where Aunt Barb criticized her mother. That would have to be redacted, somehow, if she had to surrender the book.

"I can't just hand them over," Stella countered. "They're part of my aunt's estate and I'm not the executor. Her lawyer is, and I understand there's explicit rules and regulations on what I can and cannot do in regards to her possessions." *Bit of a stretch, but Harry was in charge and he had mentioned a few things, even if he wasn't explicit.* Stella didn't think using her aunt's essential oils in the bathtub and borrowing some of her clothes to wear would be frowned upon by an American court of law, but some other things were sure to be. She made a mental note to call Harry Bernstein first thing in the morning. CYA in America couldn't be all that different from covering your arse in the UK.

"I can give you his business card and you can discuss it with him," she finished up.

"Fine." Martinez was busy making notes.

Stella turned to Carol. "Did my aunt ever mention her will to you?"

Carol shook her head. "No. Why?"

"She mentions a "Gabriel's Charities," saying she used your grandson's name."

"Gabriel? He's only three. I don't understand. Barbara never said anything to me."

"Maybe it was a spur-of-the-moment choice when she had to come up with a name then."

Carol shrugged.

"Let's get back to what happened tonight?" Martinez had written down "Gabriel's Charities" next to "Will" and underlined both words.

By the time Stella finished telling him about the rest of the events from her point of view she felt drained of energy. The bag of peas had defrosted, but the swelling was down. The painkillers were fully working on a grand scale. She yawned.

"And you?" The sergeant looked at Carol, who told him she'd been awakened by all the noise and opened her door just as the assailant was running down the stairs after battering Stella.

"Have either of you noticed any suspicious activity at the youth hostel?" He looked from one to the other.

"No," the women replied in unison.

"Barbara complained to me a couple of times when things got too noisy over there, but nothing specific or suspicious," Carol said.

I have to tell him. So, Stella did, first mentioning her aunt's journal comment about needing binoculars for a better look. "But I haven't found any around here, so I don't know if she followed through with whatever was bothering her." She reminded herself that after Olivia arrived, they needed to make a thorough search through the cupboards for the binoculars as well as the portable typewriter, plus comb through the diaries for any information that would shed light on the events that had occurred. "There is something else."

In spite of starting to look tired themselves, Sergeant Martinez and Carol both looked at her expectantly.

"I saw the brother of that dead fellow who washed up on the rocks come out of the youth hostel yesterday. I understand he was there to retrieve his brother's passport before returning to the UK."

"How do you know that?"

Martinez scribbled away as Stella gave an abbreviated explanation of how she was acquainted with Nigel and an expurgated version of them bumping into each other in Venice. She didn't lie or hold any facts back, just specific salacious parts; i.e., the shepherdess and naughty sheep phone sex bit during the transatlantic call he made to Brian. Stella wasn't a prude, but she didn't think it necessary to reveal details of someone else's sex life to total strangers. And after all, it wasn't direct evidence, she told herself.

It was getting light outside by the time the sergeant was done asking questions. Mr. Velvet hadn't moved; he was fast asleep on the dining table.

Martinez shut his notebook and stood up. "You've both been very helpful. I know it's been a long night, but I appreciate the information. I'll come back later if there's more questions–and I'm anticipating there will be. Or they might send a detective by to interview you. At any rate, you have my number," he said to Stella, and reached into his pocket to pull out a business card which he handed to Carol. "Please call if there's anything else either of you remember or think might be pertinent. Nothing is ever too small or too insignificant." He put the dining chair back by the table and moved towards the door, adding: "They'll be an officer posted outside,"

"Is that really necessary?" Carol didn't look too pleased.

"Just a precaution," Martinez assured them both.

Carol looked at the kitchen clock. "I better get ready for work if I'm taking the cat to the vet first," she told Stella. "Let me help you up."

Stella had some difficulty getting out of the armchair and onto her feet even with Carol's help.

Sergeant Martinez sprang forward to take her other arm and elbow. "Are you sure you don't need a lift to the ER right now?"

"Thanks, I really am okay. I just need some sleep."

"With a bump on the head that's not always a good idea."

"I just need to lay down."

Carol picked up the empty mug and peas, which by now had defrosted into a wet and soggy mess inside the plastic bag. "I'll be back in a while with the cat carrier. If you change your mind, I can give you a ride to the hospital or the doctor later."

"Thank you, but Olivia's coming by to stay for the weekend. She can always take me if I need to see someone."

Martinez stood aside so Carol could go back to her own apartment. When she was inside, he turned back to Stella. "Right, like I said, call if you need to."

"Is there something going on in this neighborhood, apart from the attacks on me?" she said seeing him out. "You said this was part of an ongoing investigation. Can't you tell me a bit more?"

"Not yet, but I can tell you this. The guy who tried to kill you–he wasn't acting alone. He was in cahoots with someone else close by."

CHAPTER 35

"I think the neighbors are afraid to come out of their apartments." Carol unhooked the cat carrier latch. "Nobody's out in the garden and all the doors are closed and curtains drawn."

Mr. Velvet staggered out and headed for sanctuary in a nearby closet, a plastic cone-shaped collar haloed around his neck and head so he couldn't scratch the stitches on his ear.

"He's really pissed off," she told Stella and Olivia, who were each reading one of Aunt Barb's little black books, a carafe of coffee on the table between them. "The vet examined his paw and re-bandaged it, but x-rays show his leg's not fractured and his ribs are undamaged." Carol pulled out a prescription bottle and a tube of antibiotic ointment from her jacket pocket and placed them on the table. "He's on pain meds and had an antibiotic shot, but you need to put this ointment on his paw and re-bandage it daily for a few days."

"Thanks. How much do I owe you?" Stella was shocked at the amount when Carol told her, but she'd already spoken to Harry Bernstein and he'd assured her he'd be happy to add the vet expense to the list of bills being paid.

"Barbara was very fond of that cat," he'd told her over the phone. "And considering the circumstances and that he saved your life, she'd say the plucky little fellow was worth it at any price."

He'd also insisted that both she and Olivia get head CT scans. "My cousin's a radiologist. I'll make arrangements. Don't worry about the cost," Harry had told her.

Carol said she had to get back to work. "What are you two doing with those little black books?"

"They're Aunt Barb's diaries. We're searching for any relevant information that might explain a few things, plus help the police," Stella replied.

"I didn't know she keep a diary," Carol frowned. "Let me know if you find anything; I have to go."

After Carol left, Stella made a fresh pot of coffee and she and Olivia went back to perusing the diaries. They'd already thoroughly searched the closets and cupboards for the typewriter and binoculars, but didn't find either one.

Olivia had arrived early that morning "to make sure I get a parking space close by," she'd explained to a sleepy Stella, who'd managed to lie down for a couple of hours after Sergeant Martinez departed and Carol had headed to the vet with an unhappy Mr. Velvet in the cat carrier. Parking was at a premium at the beach on weekends. Olivia had been mortified to learn of the near-fatal attack on Stella.

"I should have stayed," she'd wailed. "It might not have happened if I had."

Stella reminded her of the basement incident when she had stayed; they'd both been knocked out and bound before being stashed under the building. "No need to chastise yourself. Mr. Velvet came to the rescue."

"Brave boy!" Olivia gave a shout-out towards the partially open closet door, behind which the little black cat hid licking his wounds, before she went back to her reading.

"Oh-oh, Stella, listen to this." Olivia sat up straight and read out loud: *"I think that youth hostel's a meeting place for a drug exchange. There's a lot of young people coming and going with backpacks, which isn't suspicious on the face of it, but I saw Liz over there. I spied her through the window with my binoculars and got a close-up this morning; she was counting out money to a young guy who handed her a small packet of what I bet is cocaine, since I saw her dip her pinkie in and sample it."*

"When is that entry dated?"

Olivia turned back a page. "The first of this year."

"Anything else?"

Olivia scanned the next page. "Nothing yet. Just poetic comments about a rainstorm and the Boardwalk being flooded down by Westminster." Olivia skipped two more pages. "She's done a few sketches of stormy skies over the beach. Ah, here we go. *'People's personal consumption is their own business, but I won't have any drug dealing going on connected to this apartment building. I don't care for some of Liz's showbiz friends, including that young lawyer. I'm changing my will. And my lawyer. I'll give Harry Bernstein a call instead. He's reliable.'"* Olivia read silently for a moment. "Then she mentions you."

Stella perked up. "Let me see."

Olivia handed the book over.

"'I could make my niece my beneficiary,'" Stella read out loud. *"'But I'd like to meet her first. I haven't seen her since she was a baby. She might turn out to be just like my sister, Sheila, but she is family. And she's the only one who sent a Christmas card to*

wherever I was living after she grew up. Maybe I'll invite Stella and her boyfriend to come and stay for a vacation.'"

"So that's why my aunt called to wish me a Happy Birthday and suggested a visit," Stella grew thoughtful. "She decided to suss me out!"

"Don't be so cynical," Olivia admonished. "She might have really wanted to meet you anyway."

"That's true," Stella replied, turning a few more pages, then reading: "'*All done. I called Harry and asked him to draw up my will. Didn't mention the other one about Gabriel Charities. Just stuck it at the back of the file now it's moot.*'"

Stella reached for the phone. "Bernstein needs to know this stuff in the diary for the court, too. Then I'm calling Martinez."

CHAPTER 36

A few days later, they sat around the ironwork table on the garden patio as Sergeant Martinez gave them an update. He and Stella sported shiners on their foreheads that matched the purple bougainvillea blooming overhead. Carol, Olivia and Cindy shared a bottle of wine with Stella. Little dog Percy snoozed at his mistress' feet; Carol's cat, Pumpkin, sat on her lap, one eye on Percy. Everyone else was absent. Greg had departed to his cabin in the mountains north of Los Angeles to mourn his pet in solitude. Bill Craven was busy taking Vi and Edna to doctors' appointments. Harry Bernstein was busy in court proving Stella was Barbara Smith's rightful beneficiary. Sam had gone to visit friends and avoid the police, and the VA worker in the other front apartment was staying at his girlfriend's. The sky was blue, the sun shone brightly high above, and a gentle sea breeze rustled the leaves of the verdant foliage surrounding the patio.

Liz had been arrested, her apartment searched and Auntie Barb's typewriter and binoculars found. Gary had taken his mother to visit relatives in Ventura for a few days. He was heartbroken to find out that Liz' main occupation was not actress or waitress, but criminal.

"Once they caught up with her, she spilled the beans on everything," Martinez was saying. "Your assailant," he nodded at Stella, "was her boyfriend."

"Ah." Stella remembered the man she'd seen Liz arguing with near the Venice Canals. No wonder he'd looked slightly familiar after she'd had time to think about it.

"He was also Andrea's husband and a law student who couldn't pass the Bar exam," Martinez explained further, referring to his notebook.

"I saw them together at a café on the Boardwalk." Stella now recalled.

"He was cheating on Andrea with Liz, who he started going out with after seeing her in an acting showcase in Van Nuys. He lied to her saying he was planning to be an entertainment lawyer, which sounded like catnip to her ears." Martinez paused. "After your aunt's husband died, during a conversation with Liz she'd made an off-hand remark that when she died, any money left should go to worthy causes, naming a few charities. Hence the first will and also when Liz and her new boyfriend started plotting on how to relieve Barbara of her money. They got greedy."

Stella felt sad. She'd liked Liz.

"We know all this because it's in your aunt's diary. Incidentally, Harry Bernstein is providing us with certain pages for the criminal case." Martinez grinned. "And don't worry, he'll be redacting any personal references to your family. Only the judge will be handed the whole diary to peruse and be satisfied the pertinent pages presented are from your aunt's little black book."

Olivia wriggled her eyebrows at Stella. She'd managed to read some juicy gossip about Sheila before Stella had snatched that diary away from her.

The sergeant continued on with his summary. "So Andrea's husband intentionally introduced himself to Barbara at one of Liz's theater parties and he helped your aunt with the will. At the time he was working at a law firm contingent on his passing the Bar. However, it was done off the books, so to speak, and without that law firm's knowledge."

"Where does Andrea fit in with all of this?" Cindy topped up wineglasses. Martinez, although in plainclothes because this was his day off, was not drinking.

"She and her husband were having marriage problems for a long time due to both of their extramarital affairs, but Andrea was innocent about Liz and her husband, and didn't have anything to do with the will. She'd known Sam way back from high school; they'd dated a few times before going their separate ways after graduation. Andrea eventually got married. Sam and Liz became an item for a couple of years. Andrea separated from her husband, met up with Sam again at a club, and eventually moved into the empty apartment next to his, downstairs from your aunt. Sam and Liz broke up."

"It's a telenovela," Olivia muttered.

"Certainly is." Stella was off of pain meds, but the wine was going down well with her lingering soreness. Both she and Olivia had had their CT head scans courtesy of Harry Bernstein's radiologist cousin, and both had been given a clean bill of health, which Olivia had declared nothing short of a miracle. Stella wondered if the police knew about bird-call-man on the bike. Or any others Andrea might be involved with during the separation from her husband. Probably.

"Andrea and her husband were also having financial problems since he couldn't pass the Bar and get a decent job. Liz was, too. When an old friend came to visit her from back East, he brought a healthy supply of drugs along to consume, or otherwise share via direct sales, during his vacation. The youth hostel owner where her friend was staying was not adverse to illegal smoking or imbibement of any other sort by anyone staying there. In fact, some of his customers probably paid for their stay with some spliffs or a little baggie of cocaine or pills. Andrea's husband and Liz made him a proposition aka bribed him for their silence about not alerting the authorities, and the hostel became a way station for small amounts of drugs moving in and out of there very quickly.

There was always a certain amount of heroin use amongst some people in Venice, but with wealthier people moving in that drug of choice became cocaine which costs twice as much and is far more deadly. The young English guy who washed up near the Marina, was financing his journey across America by transporting small amounts in his backpack. Liz and company were taking a cut and setting up a network. Some of the young people doing this may not have realized the extent of this fledgling enterprise, only that 'their' drugs could be used as currency on an individual basis, not that it was part of a bigger plan. They were out in the world on an adventure and had found a way to pay for it along the way."

Stella thought of Nigel's nineteen-year-old brother, and felt sorry for the pair of them. Neville hadn't realized where an easy solution to running out of money could lead to.

Martinez continued: "Liz was getting greedy as well as desperate. Her career was going nowhere, she was getting older–for this town– and she disliked being a waitress. Both she and Andrea's husband needed a lot more money ASAP. She encouraged Neville to go swimming at night while at the same time saying it was prohibited, which only made it more enticing to the young guy. She knew rip tides could be a risk, but didn't bother to mention it because she saw a chance to steal the cocaine he had in his backpack."

"She murdered him!" Cindy was shocked.

"Not technically. She says she warned him."

"But she knew." Carol said.

"Yes."

Stella agreed with Carol and Cindy. It was a form of murder.

Martinez looked at Stella. "I want to thank you for being suspicious about your aunt's slip and fall. Liz told us the whole story.

Barbara saw them go out on the beach together. She'd been out with a friend, came back late and was watering her plants on the back porch. She'd previously seen both Liz and Neville over at the youth hostel and was putting two and two together at what was going on over there, as her diary supports. It's dark out on the beach by the water, but courtesy of the Boardwalk street lighting, your aunt saw Liz come back alone and dump the guy's clothing and backpack in a trash can after retrieving a package from it, which she correctly surmised to be drugs. The fog hadn't drifted in yet; the patio lights were off, but Liz panicked when saw Barbara watching her. There was dim lighting from the street light on Speedway, too; she thought your aunt had seen everything. Liz and Barbara had already exchanged words over your aunt's suspicions about the youth hostel. Liz confronted her. Your aunt threatened to go to the police. Liz saw her hopes of making money from her latest enterprise dry up and disappear. In a fit of pique she pushed Barbara, who fell down the stairs to her death. Then Liz realized the chance to grab your aunt's investment through Gabriel's Charities via the will."

"Another murder, another 'accident,'" Carol muttered sadly.

"But you turned up." Martinez looked at Stella.

"That night I arrived. I was at the mailboxes, wondering where my aunt's apartment was, and Liz came in. She had a restaurant waitperson's uniform on, the black jeans and tee shirt. I thought she'd just come home from work."

"She had. From an earlier shift," Martinez said. "She just hadn't changed yet."

"It's surprising no-one heard anything out there in the night," Olivia spoke up suddenly.

"Why would they?" Cindy answered. "The sound of the ocean lulls us all to sleep. Even the vagrants pass out early."

"Was it Liz that tried to run me down in the supermarket parking lot?" Stella asked Martinez?

The sergeant nodded. "By chance she saw you there. Liz knew where the spare key was to your aunt's apartment. She told Andrea's husband to go in and check to make sure the will was in the filing cabinet even though she already had a copy. She counted on you not having gone through your aunt's business files yet, and had no idea Barbara had made another will."

"The new will wasn't in the filing cabinet. I'd taken it with me to my appointment with Mr. Bernstein," Stella said.

Martinez nodded. "Andrea's husband discovered Harry Bernstein had filed the new will naming you as beneficiary, so he and Liz changed the date on the old one naming Gabriel's

Charities and filed that, plotting to kill you, although that was proving harder than expected."

"After all, Liz had already had success with two people." Stella said dryly.

"Three," Martinez said.

"Did she also kill Andrea?" Cindy was clearly upset.

Sergeant Martinez nodded. "Andrea had decided to go back to her husband. Liz was furious. They argued and ended up in a shoving match by the wooden pilings out on the sand one night."

"That sculpture thing?" Stella asked.

"Yeah, Parks and Recreation decided to arrange some old telephone poles so kids could clamber over them or joggers sit and rest, "Carol replied.

"Or dogs could pee against them," Cindy interjected in a slurred voice. All eyes turned to Percy.

"Anyway," Martinez continued. "Liz hit Andrea, who fell against the wooden pilings grouped out there and hit her head, which killed her. Liz then threw sand over her body in a half-hearted cover-up attempt."

"Who knew Liz had such a temper?" Cindy said. "She always seemed so nice."

"She was to me," Stella agreed.

"She was an actress," Carol stated flatly.

"Acting's a noble profession," Stella pointed out.

"Not in Hollywood, it's not." Carol answered.

"She was a liar," Olivia stated flatly.

"Did Andrea's husband know Liz killed her?" Stella asked Martinez.

"No. Liz deceived him, too. He thought it was some sort of jealous lover's quarrel with someone she was seeing. He's heartbroken."

"A heartbroken attempted murderer. That's really something," Olivia said.

"Why did he try to kill me?" Stella was curious. "Why him and not Liz, since she was so successful at it?"

"Number one, she told him too." Sergeant Martinez said. "With you out of the way, they thought they could get the apartment building after changing the date on their copy of the old will. Beach front property is worth a lot of money. Number two: Liz doesn't climb trees. She's afraid of heights."

"Who knew?" Cindy's voice was slurring now.

"Everyone has their Achilles heel," Sergeant Martinez said simply.

Stella was thoughtful. "Was it the boyfriend or Liz who knocked out Olivia and myself?"

"And stuck us under the building," Olivia pointed out.

"Yeah, bound and gagged."

Martinez nodded. "Both. Then he went to retrieve his vehicle while she waited, hiding in the garden. They planned to dump your bodies in the Venice Canals, but Bill Craven turned up."

"I'm still surprised no-one heard anything," Stella said.

"I'm glad Bill turned up when he did," Olivia said. "I know he'd come back to check on his aunties, but what was so important about the old suitcase he needed to retrieve from the basement?"

Stella smiled. "I've asked him about that. He said it contained old love letters." What she didn't say was that he'd confessed Mrs. Edwards and he had been lovers many, many years ago, and corresponded when he'd gone back to sea.

Martinez made a note in his little notebook. He'd known about Bill turning up, but not why, Stella realized. Then her thoughts turned back to Nigel with his dead brother. And Brian. They'd need a lot of TLC. *Everyone needs more tender loving care.* She vowed to put time into repairing things between the three of them. *But I need to recover from all this a bit more first.*

The others were finishing up their wine.

"I have another question," Stella said. "Since I was the one who became violently ill more than anyone else after my aunt's funeral, did Liz try and poison me?"

"She did," Martinez told her.

"How?"

"The sangria, the apple slices floating on top."

Stella remembered Liz topping her glass up. "But others were drinking it, too."

Sergeant Martinez smiled. "Apparently, you drank more of it than anyone else. She made sure of that."

Dammit! I'm giving up drinking. Stella looked at her current empty wineglass. *Or at least cutting back.*

Martinez concluded his notes, then looked around. "Where's your cat, Stella? Where's our real hero of the hour?"

So, it was no longer 'Ms. Maris.' "He's in recovery," she replied.

Mr. Velvet remained in the closet to maintain his dignity, which had forced Stella to temporarily place a cat litter box in the bathroom. At the back of her mind Velvet the Lionheart had become Velvet the Conehead, but she couldn't blame him for retreating to lick his wounds. She was hand-feeding him tidbits of salmon stuffed with pain meds for dinner and anything else he wanted.

There was one more thing Stella wanted to know. "Where's Ron's son in all of this? Is he still around?"

"No, he went back to Toronto," Martinez replied. "The detectives followed up on that info you gave me. He had nothing to do with these events."

An audible rustle in the bushes made Percy perk up and Pumpkin give a frightened little squeak. All heads turned towards the swaying foliage and leaves. A fluffy white head appeared, surveying them all. The rest of the body followed, then sauntered nonchalantly towards Greg's apartment as everyone stared in disbelief.

Cindy was the first to break the silence. "Oh, shit. Hitler's back!"

ABOUT THE TYPE

The title font is Timberline, designed with felt brush pen by Giuseppe Salerno of Torino, Italy and Paco González, from Valencia. The design conveys the distinct featues of the influential cities of Berlin, Madrid, Torino and Valencia. The interior text is set in Calluna, designed by Jos Buivenga, and combines the charm of classic design with the clean-cut appeal of modernism.

www.ingramcontent.com/pod-product-compliance
Lightning Source LLC
Chambersburg PA
CBHW041043310726
48978CB00011BA/417